HAWK

MEN OF BIRD'S EYE BOOK ONE

KAT SAVAGE

D1520474

For every single mom,
for every person starting over,
and for all of those certain you'll never love again.
Your Hawk is somewhere, distracted by the wrong women.
But he'll come to his senses and find you.
He'll be a fucking psycho.
So don't be afraid to be his straitjacket.

PENIS ENVY

HAWK

I watch a blonde girl twirl her hair around her finger then pop her gum. She points at a tiny dick with a smiley face and nods vigorously at her brunette friend. Her equally annoying friend laughs and points out the heart-shaped scrotum.

"It's perfect," the blonde says between giggles.

She's fucking kidding, right?

I turn back to my sketch because far be it from me to pass judgment on what this barely legal girl is going to get permanently inked onto her body. But why she'd pick a fucking smiling dick with a ball sack is still beyond me and I'm inclined to believe that's less judgmental and more like plain common sense.

You don't tattoo genitals on your body. You just don't.

While I'm lost in tiny cartoon scrotum thoughts and shading in the eyes of a mysterious woman I'm sketching, Will interrupts me.

"Hey, man. Sorry, but I need you on this one," she says.

Will is short for Willette. She's been my best friend since fourth grade, and she manages Bird's Eye Tattoo Studio.

I look past her to the counter where the aforementioned blonde is standing, admiring her dick flash, and I immediately start shaking my head. "No way. That's a job for Hanson," I say.

"Yeah, I know. But he's running late." She looks at me, pleading hope in her eyes.

If it were anyone but Will, I would tell them to fuck off. I throw my pencil down and close my sketchbook. "Fine."

"Great. I'll send her back," she says.

All business with Will. That's why she's my shop manager.

I'm pouring ink and laying out needles when my client clears her throat behind me.

"Hey there!" she says, all too enthusiastically for my liking.

"Sit here," I instruct, waiting as she takes a seat.

She looks up at the sign above my head that displays my name. "Wow, is Hawk your real name?" she asks, twirling her hair again.

I hear the snap of her gum at the end of her sentence and I want to tell her to spit it out but I don't.

"Yep," I say for the twentieth time this week. *Mind you, it's only Wednesday.*

"That's so cool. My name is Rebecca. My friends call me Becky." She leans in closer to me and pushes her arms together so her tits push up and out.

It's not that I don't like tits. *Who doesn't love tits?* I just don't like Rebecca's tits.

"Where do you want this dick?"

"What?" she asks, flustered.

I hold up the flash stencil of the smiling scrotum cartoon she'd chosen mere moments ago. It seems her attempted flirting and my *so cool* name has sidetracked her.

"Oh, right! Right here," she says. She unbuttons the top of her pants and tugs them down a little, turning on her side to give me her hip.

This girl is about to get a smiling dick and balls tattooed on her hip. This is not why I became a tattoo artist.

I put my earbuds in, assuring Rebecca I do my best work when I'm focused. I've found that clients don't tend to argue when risking their skin, and it's an easy way for me to avoid the mind-numbing chatter they try to spit my way. I slap on my black nitrile gloves and watch Rebecca watching my arm muscles flex.

Then, I get to work.

I lay the stencil, dip the needle, step on the pedal, and the familiar buzz of my machine fills any silence the music doesn't.

As my hand vibrates up and down the lines of the cartoon cock, I study the body language between Rebecca and her nameless friend and wonder how she arrived at this moment. How she got here, getting this tattoo.

What life choice brought you here, Rebecca? Why are you ruining your future sex life with a tiny smiling peen?

I'm just speaking for myself here, but no way am I sleeping with a woman who has a fucking dick and balls tattooed on her.

I make quick work of the fairly simple tattoo and remove the earbuds once I'm finished. Just in time to overhear her friend tell her how funny this is and how they'll be laughing about it for years to come.

No, Rebecca. No, you won't.

And I'm not going to lie, her friend is kind of a shitty friend. You're supposed to talk friends out of terrible life decisions, not encourage ones that will completely stunt their sex life. I'm guessing there will be a cover-up or removal scheduled in eigh-teen months or less.

I walk the girls to the front after we wrap up, giving Rebecca the care instruction sheet before passing her off to Will at the front counter to process her payment.

Rebecca leans in close and hands me a wad of cash. "There's a little extra tip in there," she says, winking at me quite conspicuously.

I thank her and turn back toward my booth, careful not to give her any indication that her wink was welcome. As I unfold the cash to put it in my wallet, I realize Rebecca's phone number is written on a slip of paper inside. I separate it from the cash and stare at it for a moment. The girl's got balls. *Literally and figu-ratively now*, I remind myself.

"Looks like you got another one," Avery says.

"You want it?" I flip it around, showing it to my fellow tattoo artist across from me. His shaved head is the only almost-menacing thing about him. That, and he keeps trying to get everyone to call him *Spider*. I guess he doesn't think Avery is edgy enough for this lifestyle.

"No thanks. I like to have the only dick in bed," he says.

Poor Rebecca. I have a feeling Avery won't be the last man to have such an opinion. I crumple up the little slip of paper and throw it into the waste basket. *I don't have time for that.*

I clean up my space, directing my attention back to my sketch. The woman I'm drawing has warm eyes and light hair. Her lips are pressed into a line and I haven't decided if it's sad or not. I keep dreaming about her. In my dream, I never reach her in time to find out. I get so close and then I'm waking up, left wondering.

"Sorry I'm late!" Hanson bursts in the back door and I shoot him a look. Hanson isn't a full-time artist yet, only an apprentice. He's also so young he doesn't know the boy band Hanson, making him an easy target for jokes and jabs.

"You'll have to take it up with Will," I say, cocking an eyebrow at him.

He gulps. Hanson is scared to death of Will the way Catholic kids fear nuns with rulers. He sets his backpack down in his booth, hanging his head low as he sulks off to find her. After accepting Rebecca's payment, Will hustled to the back somewhere, likely the office.

His fears aren't unfounded. She'll have him stocking shelves all day for this. Will takes no shit. I have a slight advantage of knowing her so long, so she doesn't affect me the way she does Hanson and Avery.

When you've been someone's friend long enough that you were there for their first period—which they got at your house just before crying on your shoulder—they just don't strike as much fear in you.

I check the clock and see the day is winding down. I stretch back in my chair, rolling my shoulders and neck. Being hunched over all day really does a number on your body. I finish a few more lines of my sketch and put it away so I can wrap up cleaning the rest of my space. After grabbing my jacket and keys, I start to walk toward the back.

"Hey, Hawk?" Will's voice calls to me from somewhere in the storage room.

I shift my weight to change trajectory and slip inside, looking around. Her shoulder-length purple hair bobs up and down behind a shelf as I step toward her.

"What's up?" I ask.

"Don't forget we have that guy coming tomorrow to interview for the front desk position. Do you want to meet him? Interview him?" she asks.

"I don't care. I trust you," I say.

She huffs. She hates when I'm dismissive.

"Look, if I'm around, I'll make a show. If I'm not, I'm not," I say.

"Fine," she says.

We nod at each other—our unspoken way of saying goodbye.

"See you tomorrow." I head out the back door and immediately to the stairs. *Yes, I am the cliché tattoo shop owner who lives in a loft above his tattoo shop.*

When I put it that way, it sounds awful. But when I say *I'm a successful small business owner who owns the building his business is housed in and lives in the spacious loft apartment above it*, it sounds better.

I unlock the door and walk into my place of solace, greeted by the love of my life. The only bitch I care about. *Well, almost.*

"Hi, baby girl. Did you miss me?" I say in a soft, playful tone.

My two-year-old black pitbull, Raven, stretches and leisurely leaps from the couch.

It's a less than enthusiastic greeting, but I take what I can get.

NO REST FOR THE WEARY
DREW

I'm going to throw up. I'm going to throw up because I'm going to be late and I hate being late. I fly down the busy sidewalk as quickly as I can. I didn't calculate the early morning commuters, the foot traffic, or the time it would take to navigate any of this correctly. Louisville, Kentucky isn't nearly as big as Philly, but this area in particular is much busier than I expected.

"Momma, slow down!" Ava says.

"I wish I could, sweetheart!" I call back to her. At this point, I'm practically dragging her behind me by her hand. I hear her feet shuffling to keep up with me and I'm certain if I try to speed up any more, I'll cause her to trip and fall.

We round the corner and I see the sign for the place. *Almost there. Just a little farther.* Of course, then I have to figure out what to do with Ava while I interview. While I realize it isn't exactly *professional* to bring a child with you to an interview, I don't really have a choice.

She doesn't start school until Monday because her transcripts are delayed. And, considering she's only eight, she's too young to stay home by herself. So, I had to bring her with me.

I slow down as we make it to the entrance and look up at the sign. Bird's Eye Tattoo Studio has a menacing bird skull logo and the look on Ava's face says it all. *Are you really going to work here?*

The **HELP WANTED** sign is still in the window, but hopefully not for much longer. My heart sinks as I lower my eyes and see the additional sign that reads **NO MINORS ALLOWED**. I shouldn't be surprised, of course. That's pretty normal for tattoo studios. But now I'm panicking. I look down at Ava, who's panting, chest heaving as she catches her breath.

There's parking for the building on the side, and I follow it around to the back entrance as instructed. There, I see a small patio with some benches and a picnic table under an awning right in front of the large windows. It's pretty quiet back here—and private.

I have no choice. I turn to Ava. "Okay, sit right here and don't move. Don't talk to anyone. I'll be right inside there. I'll be keeping an eye on you the entire time."

"Okay." She plops down on the bench before taking out her sketchpad and pencil, clearly unperturbed by the situation.

"Wish me luck!" I say, stepping toward the door, but she doesn't. Ava doesn't hear me. Not after the sketchpad and pencil is out. She doesn't see or hear anything after that.

I walk in and make my way through the shop, toward what I'm guessing is technically the front. I glance back, relieved I can still see Ava through the window from here.

"What can I do for you?" a woman with fading purple hair and piercing brown eyes asks from behind the front counter.

"My name is Drew Ashby. I have an interview for the front

desk receptionist position. I think I'm supposed to ask for Will?" I say, my shoulders straightening with each word.

"Oh, holy shit, that's me," the petite woman says.

Oh okay. Will is a woman. "Oh, hello," I say, extending my hand for her to shake.

"So Drew is a woman?" she asks.

"And Will is a woman," I confirm, conspiratorially.

"Touché," she says, laughing and nodding. It would appear we've both been thrown for a loop by our unconventional gender-neutral names. *This is what we get for only communicating by email until now.*

"Let's head back to the office," she says.

"I'm sorry, I hate to do this, but is it at all possible for us to interview in your back lobby?" I ask.

"Oh, sure," she says without question.

I fully expected to have to explain my predicament, but she takes my request in stride and I feel a surge of relief as we walk that way.

We take a seat on the couch in the back, right in front of the window, and I am mere inches from Ava. I breathe easier knowing I can interview with her in my line of sight.

"So, why do you want the job?" Will asks.

"Well, I just moved here from Philly. I'm recently divorced. The only family member I have left was living here, but she decided about a week ago—right after I arrived—that it was time for her to do some traveling. So now, it's just me and my daughter." I point out the window to the back of Ava's head, watching Will's eyes widen as she begins to understand my situation.

"Have you ever worked in a tattoo shop before?" she asks.

"No, but I've had other front desk positions in the past and

I'm confident I could catch on quickly," I say, trying hard not to let my voice crack. "And, if I'm being *totally* honest, this place is in walking distance from me, and the divorce left me without a car."

Will studies me, looking me up and down. "Do you have any tattoos yourself?" She raises her eyebrow at me, a smirk falling over her lips.

The question throws me off. "Um, only one." My answer comes out more like an admission.

"What's it of?" she asks.

"Just the outline of a bird," I say.

She nods, as if she's letting that response sink in more than any other I've given.

"Listen, I need this job. I need to provide for my daughter. I get the impression her father won't be helping all that much, and I'm just doing the best I can. I was sort of pushed rather unexpectedly into single parenthood a few months ago. I'm not here to make waves, drastic changes, or even friends if you don't want. Just money to provide for her," I admit, fully aware of the desperation in my tone.

I look lovingly out at Ava, who's still doodling away on her sketchpad.

Will nods. "I see. Well, the job is yours if you want it. If you do, you can start Monday. Why don't you have her come inside and sit so I can show you around?"

My eyes brighten, immediately tearing up. "Thank you. So much." I nod and swallow, suppressing the emotion I'm feeling from this simple act of kindness on her part. Then, I go get Ava.

We leave Ava sitting on the same couch we'd been sitting on

while Will takes me to fill out some paperwork and show me around.

This is good. Things are looking up. *Finally.* From destitute to having a job in a week's time isn't bad. Now if I can just keep this sort of track record, maybe I can give Ava some sort of a decent life. Her father sure as hell doesn't seem concerned with any of it.

It's up to me. Just me. And I can do it. *I think.*

PARDON ME

HAWK

The front doorbell rings overhead as I enter the shop, swiping at the spot of mustard I got on my shirt at lunch. I fucking hate stains. I hate spots. I know myself well enough to know I'm going to end up walking straight out the back door and upstairs to change before I go back to work.

I head toward the back lobby, noticing a small pair of legs swinging back and forth out of the corner of my eye. It's strange and distracting. I slowly turn and look up, still wiping at the mustard spot with a wet nap. There's a small human sitting on the couch by the window. *What is she, like, seven?* She's drawing a picture or something I think and bobbing her head back and forth, singing to herself, and where the fuck are her parents?

I look around the shop, but the only adults in sight are Avery and his client. The sign on the door clearly states **NO MINORS** and this is definitely a minor. I walk over to Avery's booth.

"Does she belong to your client?" I ask, my thumb hitched

over my shoulder, not bothering to ask the client directly. He shakes his head.

Where's Will? She should handle this. This feels like her territory.

"Will?" I yell back toward the office and stock room.

"Yeah?" I hear in return.

"There's something you have to handle," I call.

"Gonna have to wait," she calls back.

I walk to the back office and throw the door open. "Dude, there's a kid out there," I say, before I notice Will isn't alone.

She rolls her eyes at me the way she does when what she really wants to do is kick me in the shin. "Yeah, I know," she says, and then, "Hawk, this is Drew. Drew this is Hawk. He owns the place." She looks back to me, saying, "She's our new front desk receptionist. The kid out there is Ava, and she belongs to Drew."

Will looks at me like I've just killed a kitten, and I swallow. I look at Drew, who is looking at me. She's not smiling. She's not twirling her hair or popping her gum. She has warm eyes and light hair. Her lips are pressed into a line. The same kind of mouth I think I was sketching yesterday.

"Drew Ashby," is all she says as she extends her hand to me. Her honey eyes are clouded and I think she's pissed off at me but I'm not sure.

Nor do I really care. "I thought you were supposed to be a guy?"

Her hand stays suspended between us. "Well, I'm not."

"There aren't supposed to be any minors in here," I say.

"Won't happen again," she says, finally lowering her hand.

Drew turns back to Will and says she'll see her Monday then steps past me, walking to the back of the shop. She collects the small child and they walk through the shop and out the front door, the bell jingling overhead as they leave.

"What the fuck, Will?" I ask.

"Me? What the fuck, *you*, Hawk? Could you be a bigger dick?" Will accuses, slamming her elbow into my ribs.

I guffaw and recoil. "I thought the applicant was a dude?"

"So did I." She shrugs.

"No women are supposed to work here. You're the only exception," I say, reminding her of something we discussed a while back.

"Well, it's time for that to change. Besides, her name is Drew. It works," she says.

I shake my head, knowing no matter what I say, it's too late. I may be the owner, but I put trust and management power in Will for a reason. "Why was her kid here?"

"Ava doesn't start school until Monday, and Drew is a single mom," Will says.

"Oh." I think about my own mother. She raised me and my brother on her own and I'm pretty sure I saw my father a grand total of maybe ten times from age five up until high school graduation.

"Exactly," Will says.

I roll my eyes. Her knowing me for so long has its disadvantages, too. "Fine," I say. "But her daughter can't just be hanging out in here all the time."

Shoving my earbuds in, I sulk back to my booth and sit down, taking my sketchbook out and flipping it open.

I've lost that battle. I scratch the back of my neck, irritation crawling up my spine. Though I don't know why. *Was it Drew's clear annoyance with me? Maybe.* Or maybe I'm annoyed with myself. Maybe I'm annoyed that she was clearly annoyed with me.

I look at the tattoo of a hawk peeking out from my stained shirt, which I'd completely forgotten about. It's the tattoo I got when I finally decided to embrace my name. Now I sort of hate it a little, but it is what it is.

Why did that woman want to work here, anyway? She doesn't fit the bill. No tattoos. No piercings. She looked so normal. Not your typical tattoo shop worker. We're known for our ink, our holes, and our wild hair choices, among other things.

Last month, Will had green hair. Now it's purple. Hanson's hair was bleached last summer. I have my nose pierced. And all of us have more tattoos than we can count.

My thoughts settle on the little girl. *What was her name? Anna? Amber? No.*

Ava? Yes. Ava. She was drawing. I wonder how her mother became a single parent, where her father is, and most importantly, I wonder what she was drawing. I can't help myself. I let my thoughts get carried away as I begin to work on a custom piece for a client who's coming in next week. Eventually those thoughts circle back to my own mother.

My mother, Gail Tanner, was my savior in my youth. She's one of the best people I know. I consider myself lucky to have had such a strong, capable parent. My brother Derek and I didn't make it easy on her. We certainly had our fair share of getting into trouble and fights, not only with each other but with the other kids in the neighborhood as well.

"Hey, Hawk?" Will's voice is muffled through my music and I look up to see her leaning casually against my booth.

"What's up?" I ask, taking one of my earbuds out.

"I need a favor," she starts, and this is never good.

Whenever Will starts a conversation needing a favor, it pretty much always ends with me agreeing to do something ridiculous for her. Like, agreeing to help her move her entire apartment in one night after work because she waited until the last minute. *Did I mention we didn't have a U-Haul?*

Or the time she asked if I could watch her cat while she went out of town for the weekend with some dude she was dating, and my dog Raven almost murdered it because it wouldn't stop scratching her in the face.

Or the time she begged me to go to a costume party as the Mad Hatter and after finally agreeing, I showed up only to discover she changed her mind and went as a vampire instead of Alice.

"What do you need, Will?" I reluctantly set down my pencil, bracing myself.

"Can you come to dinner with me and my parents this weekend?" she asks, her eyes squinting and pleading.

Fuck.

WHEN THE PARTY'S OVER
DREW

When my Aunt Penny decided six days after Ava and I arrived here that she needed to travel and go sightseeing while she *still had time*, she sold almost all her possessions and left in a hurry. What remains is her small apartment with a mismatched couch and chair, a small kitchen table with one good chair and a wobbly stool, a futon in the one bedroom while the other sits completely empty, and barely enough dishes for me and Ava to use during a meal. Lots of coffee mugs, though. Got plenty of those for some reason.

Aside from that, all I have is what Ava and I had packed with us when we moved. Three suitcases of clothes, and one bag of toys and personal belongings like photos and keepsakes.

To say the place is pretty bare is a gross understatement. On the plus side, the rent is cheap, the utilities for a place this size can't be too bad, and it's in close proximity to everything I need. I spent the last bit of money I had on Ava's school uniforms—the mandatory khaki pants and polo shirts—and supplies, in addition to putting some food in the fridge. I just hope it will last us until my first paycheck.

The need for that paycheck is exactly why it's Sunday night and I'm in the kitchen packing Ava's lunch into her purple lunch box, reviewing the school bus schedule with her and how she'll take it from school to my work and then will have to wait outside in the back until I get off. Because everything *has* to go smoothly.

I have to work; there's no other option. Ava's being surprisingly calm about the whole thing while I, on the other hand, am a bundle of panic infused twine.

"Don't worry, Momma. I've taken buses before," she says.

To my relief, she'll have a fairly short bus ride to my job and will only have to wait for about an hour or so before I get off work.

"Don't talk to any strangers," I remind her. "And keep your cell phone in your backpack on silent until you get on the bus but then turn it on, okay?"

Under normal circumstances, I wouldn't have gotten her a cell phone at this age, but given we're in a new city and she'll be riding a bus, it just seemed like the only logical option. Hence, another reason I'm flat broke until I get my first paycheck.

She nods her head at me for the hundredth time this evening and I stuff her lunch box into the fridge so it's ready to go in the morning. Her uniform is hanging in her closet, and her backpack is full of school supplies. My child is prepared; I'm quite the opposite.

Anxiety swells in my throat and threatens to spill out all over the chipped yellow linoleum, but I swallow hard, forcing it back down. Part of the problem may be that I haven't eaten today. I completely forgot with the fog of today's school supply buying activities. Or maybe it was due to my anxiety induced deep clean of the apartment where I scrubbed the baseboards and tile grout in the bathroom. Either or both are a possibility.

I grab an apple from the bowl on the counter and bite into it, making a conscious effort to relax my shoulders and take a few deep breaths. *What does one wear when they work at a tattoo shop?*

Oh my Odin, I can't believe I'll be working at a tattoo shop. If my college professors could see me now.

I have a feeling that one of my nine pairs of slacks would be overdoing it. I think back to what Will was wearing—ripped black skinny jeans and a tank top. *Oh dear.* I don't know about that. I absentmindedly walk back toward the empty bedroom and slide open the closet door. It gets stuck halfway and I have to tug on it to get it to open the rest of the way.

No wonder my aunt wanted to *travel*. This place is falling apart. I flip through the clothes I brought with me and realize, aside from slacks, I have very few options. I bite down on the apple, holding it between my teeth, and slip a pair of dark denim jeans off a hanger, holding them up to my hips. I step in front of the dingy full-length mirror affixed to the back side of the bedroom door. *Not bad.* They have small rips above the knees. Nothing too over the top.

I lay them over my arm and rifle through my shirts before settling on a T-shirt with John Wick on it. *Because John Wick is cool, right? Yes, okay.* This is going to work. It has to, really. It's this or corporate business casual and I already look out of place at Bird's Eye as it is. Best not to draw more attention.

"Mom!" Ava yells from the kitchen, and I run back there to find her freaking out—crouched on the floor, ripping everything out of the once-perfectly-packed new backpack I just organized.

"What's wrong? What are you doing?" I drop to my knees to gather the items.

"My pencil broke and I can't find a new one!" Ava says this like it's a matter of life and death. And for her, perhaps it is.

I sigh, taking the bag from her frantic hands. Navigating to the pencil box, I take out two pencils and hand them to her. She hugs my neck and then scurries to her feet. I have half a mind to make her clean this up but I'm obsessive. I know she won't do it the way I want, so I do it myself. *A mother's plight.*

After her backpack is re-packed and my apple core is in the trash, I tuck her into bed, which is actually just the futon. I fold her turquoise twin comforter under her chin and kiss her forehead, savoring this moment when her eyes are closed and I can just absorb her without worry. Kids are blessings but they're also sort of assholes, and anyone with one will tell you.

I walk out to the living room and grab the linens I use from the small hall closet, plopping onto the couch, which doubles as my bed. The olive-green upholstery is not attractive or comfortable. Its itchy texture must be covered up each night with two layers of sheets. It seems Aunt Penny had an affinity for sitting on something that resembles the feel of a wire brush.

I look over at the orange-and-cream striped chair and wonder how my aunt came to own these two pieces of furniture. Then again, if I had to guess, I'd say everything in this apartment most likely came from either a flea market or secondhand shop. Not that there's anything wrong with that. It would just explain why nothing matches. I'm also certain she didn't get any of it after 1983.

I think back to my old life. My life with Curtis and our perfectly matching beige furniture. His pressed suits, neatly lined in our closet, which was probably half the size of the bedrooms in this apartment. A word to the wise: When your lawyer husband files for a divorce, you won't get anything. Not the house your daughter lives in and goes to school from. Not the furniture you helped pick out. Not the car you drive. He'll figure out a way to pay the minimum amount of child support despite making way more money and will refuse visitation of any kind.

That's probably the part that hurts the most. I don't care about the possessions, the money. I care about Ava's heart. Though she won't say it, I know it's silently broken.

I check the alarm app on my phone four times before I finally fall asleep, thoughts of Ava, Curtis, and my first day of work tomorrow swirling 'round and 'round.

SOMEONE NEW
HAWK

Despite Will's hard exterior, she's actually quite soft. Not that anyone else around here would know that. Which is why, every Monday morning, she insists on bringing donuts in for the shop. But this morning, I'm doing it. Why? Because dinner with her parents last night was the biggest shit show nightmare in the entire state. Maybe the whole region. Again, why? The short version is, her parents are and have always been assholes. The long version involves her *poor life choices* and *marking up her body,* and some other stuff I've had a front row seat to for years now.

Some people think we're fucking, but we're not. We would never. I can't. She can't. It's way too weird to even think about. There's never even been a time we've considered it.

I round the corner to the shop—three boxes of donuts balancing in one hand while I try to fish for my keys in my pocket with the other—and I stop when I see Drew standing in front of it. *Oh, right. She starts today. Why is she so early?*

She checks her watch and looks down the sidewalk in the

opposite direction, then back my way and a look of recognition crosses her face. Her shoulders straighten just a smidge as her body twists toward me. I'm still a few paces off and take these few moments to assess her in a way I hadn't when she was in the shop the other day.

To the best of my ability, without raising awareness, my eyes skate up her legs. Her sculpted thighs and thick hips taper into a proportionate waist. Her tits are...impressive. Really impressive. Unlike Rebecca's, I'm okay looking at these. Her pale skin is not tattooed, and this throws me off. Not in a bad way, necessarily. But it still makes me wonder how she came to want to work at a tattoo shop.

She's wearing a John Wick T-shirt and I support that, because a man who kills for his dog is pretty fucking cool in my book. Her blonde hair falls over her shoulders and she's obviously used some kind of contraption to put waves in it.

As I draw closer, I notice the smattering of freckles over her cheeks. The pale pink of her lips. But mostly, I notice the way the light catches and illuminates the soft honey color of her irises. For a moment, I forget I'm supposed to be unlocking the door.

Until she speaks.

"Do you want me to help you with those?" She holds out her hands.

I shuffle the boxes of donuts to her, careful not to make skin-to-skin contact, though I don't know why. Propping the door of the shop open for her, I nod for her to step in first.

"You can put the donuts on the front counter. Willette will be in from the back in a few minutes to show you where they go," I say.

"Will?" Drew asks.

"Yeah, Will. Sorry, it's short for Willette." I head back to the stock room and grab a few things I need for my booth.

When I come out, Drew is flipping through posters of flash on the wall. She seems intrigued and almost appreciative of the art. From the corner of my eye, I watch her stop on a sheet full of constellations. It seems like she's looking for something specific. Her eyes narrow as her fingers trace over one. Just as I'm turning to see what's caught her eye, I hear a familiar but grumpy voice.

"Is the coffee on yet?" Will asks. The back door slams shut behind her. "And how come we have to be here a half hour before the shop opens and before those other two fucks have to come in?" She makes a hitchhiking thumb over her shoulder at Avery and Hanson's chairs.

"Do you want to deal with them longer than you have to?" I ask.

"Good point," she says, pressing the button to start the coffee machine.

"Drew is here." I nod toward her.

"Perfect," Will says. "Hey, Drew? Come on over. Have some coffee." She holds a mug out toward our new employee, who abandons the flash she was looking at to join us.

I push my earbuds in as Will takes over to explain where the donuts are displayed and how we always have fresh coffee and so on. She shows Drew the stock room, where we keep all the front desk supplies. I take my earbuds out intermittently, hearing Will tell Drew how she'll now be the one restocking the booth supplies when the front desk is slow, and to make sure she occasionally asks me and the guys if we need anything.

"Oh, and this," Will adds. "This down here is the cash box." She pulls out the petty cash box we keep under the front desk.

"We keep it here for emergencies. It's for the employees to pull from and use. We also donate to it. Well, mostly Hawk donates to it. But yeah, you work here now, so if you need it, take it." Will opens it to show her.

Drew's eyebrows draw up. "You mean like, pay it back later?"

"Not necessarily," Will says. "If you're short on cash before payday or have an emergency, or even just need a soda and don't have cash on you, that's what it's here for. If you want to pay it back, go ahead. But it's not required." Will shrugs her shoulders, while Drew looks genuinely perplexed.

I smirk but I don't know why. Providing the cash box is something I'm proud to do for my employees.

The back door opens and shuts, and with it comes the shuffling sounds of not one but two sets of feet.

"Dude, yes," Avery says.

"No way, dude," Hanson says.

"I'm telling you, I totally fucked her," Avery says confidently.

I roll my eyes because *what in the actual fuck*.

"Excuse me?" Will says, standing square shouldered at the front counter, now facing their way, clearly not amused at their choice in conversation topics.

Drew's face is burning bright pink next to her. The guys look like deer caught in headlights and I lean against my booth to watch this unfold, because I wouldn't miss Will giving them an ass chewing for all the world.

I'll be interested to see how Drew handles all of the shenanigans that go on in this place. Between Avery and Hanson's often crude banter, Will's strong presence, and my quiet demeanor that borders on asshole territory, I don't think she'll last.

COMPREHENSIVE EVALUATION
DREW

Aside from Will giving Avery and Hanson six different kinds of hell first thing this morning, my first day at work has been fairly easy. I've answered calls. Most of which I've had to put on hold while finding out the answers from Will but that was to be expected. She fully intended it to be that way, as we agree learning by doing is the best method. She gave me access to the electronic calendar of appointments, which was fairly simple to learn, and I've been inputting those for the artists as well.

Everyone at Bird's Eye seems really nice. Will is actually one of the sweetest people I've ever met. Not that you could tell by looking at her. I get the impression that when people first meet her, they think she's rigid. I'm sure she can be, but it's not her default.

She's got anchors tattooed on her chest. Her arms are covered. As is some of her back, from what I could tell. Her ears have several holes in each, and I think her tongue is pierced too. On the two occasions I've seen her, she's worn mostly black.

Avery and Hanson seem nice enough, too. They're younger, chattier, and vibrant, with easygoing dispositions. They don't really seem to take anything too seriously.

And Hawk...

He seems, at the very least, neutral. Maybe that's not the right word. Cordial? Indifferent? Professional? Yeah, maybe one of those. Although, he was sort of rude the other day. I can't really figure him out.

Over the course of today, I've noticed him looking at me a few times. Every time I had my back to him while performing a task, I swear it was like I could *feel* his eyes on me. Heat would creep up the back of my neck and my hands would start shaking. I'd whirl around as nonchalantly as I could, and each time, he'd divert his eyes.

Perhaps it's just because I'm new. Maybe it's because he can't figure out what someone like me would be doing in a place like this when I clearly don't fit.

Whatever the reason, his gaze is rather unsettling.

Maybe it's his menacing electric blue eyes or the way they contrast his nearly jet-black hair and pale skin. Maybe it's his devastating jaw or the way his mouth is always pressed into a nearly perfect straight line. Or that he's covered in tattoos and I want to examine all of them. Or maybe it's his devastating jaw. *Wait, I already said that.*

You know what, it doesn't matter. Technically, he's my boss.

I'm pretty sure he thinks I'm weird or maybe he hates me. I have no idea. And even if all that weren't true, I'm still riding the divorce train and I'm not stopping for the next several stations.

My eyes flutter to the clock on the wall. I hadn't noticed so much of the day was already behind me. *Just another hour before I get off.* I make my way to the back lobby to check for Ava, and I'm just in time to see her arrive. A small sigh of relief escapes me.

Ava waves to me, then sits down on the bench and takes out her sketchbook. I smile, glad she successfully made it here on the bus without any issues. I hate that she has to sit out there on that bench every day for an hour until I get off, but there's not much I can do about it.

As I make my way back to the front counter, I remind myself it could always be worse. Though I may have to think of a new plan soon, because there's no way I'll let her sit out there in the winter. I just pray there are no rainy days anytime soon.

"So, are you into astrology?" Hawk's voice interrupts my thoughts, startling me, and I drop the stack of papers I was holding. They scatter onto the floor. *Great.*

"Shit, I'm sorry. What?" I ask as I kneel.

He kneels too, collecting the stray sheets closer to him. "I saw you looking at the constellations on the wall."

"Oh, um, I guess I like them, yeah," I say, my voice less sure than I intend.

Hawk is unnerving—for many reasons.

"Which one?" he asks.

"I like Orion," I say.

"You should get it."

We stand as Hawk places the forms on top of the stack in my hands, his fingers brushing the sensitive skin at my wrists.

"I don't know." I shrug. "I guess it would make a good second tattoo."

"What's the one you have now?" he asks.

"The outline of a bird."

I watch Hawk's eyes search me, search my body like he's trying to work out a riddle. And I feel tingly.

"Where?" he asks.

"On my thigh." I point down. "Right here."

Is it fucking hot in here all of a sudden? My chest is warm, no doubt pink and splotchy. His eyes travel the length of my body to where I'm pointing, and I don't like this. This isn't right. I turn back to the counter, reorganizing the papers I'd dropped.

"Where would you get Orion?" he asks.

I pause shuffling the papers to consider his question. "Maybe on my collarbone? I'm not sure. I haven't really given it any thought."

"Let me know if you decide. We tattoo each other for free when we don't have appointments," he says.

Then he walks away just as quickly as he'd interrupted and flustered me.

Rubbing the warmth from my chest, I finish with these damn papers while giving his offer some thought. Then, I push it as far out of my mind as I can. Because if I'm unnerved when he hands me papers, I'm not sure having him stab me repeatedly with a needle is a good idea.

He's sort of cold and blasé about everything. He never cracks a smile or makes any sort of facial expressions beyond his signature neutral flat-line lips. We had a rude encounter the other day, then he barely talked to me all day today, and now he's offering to tattoo me? *What?* Strange. His new word is *strange.*

Indifferent and strange.

I check my watch and realize this ordeal has pushed me close enough to time to leave that I should go find Will. I check on Ava through the window as I head back to the office to discuss my day with Will, what tomorrow will consist of, and if anything needs to change or improve.

Awkward but sort of hot moments between me and Hawk aside, I'm so stoked about today. I think it went well. Hell, I'm just relieved and elated to be working in general. I do the mental math as I slip out the door toward Ava, calculating if I can afford an ice cream treat for the two of us before we go home. After all, we should celebrate surviving our first official day—her at school, me here.

Still, as I take her by the hand, leading her away from Bird's Eye, I can't help but replay each moment I found Hawk staring at me.

I haven't felt heat like that in a long time. Possibly ever.

HEY, ASSHOLE

HAWK

T alking to Drew was a mistake. I realized that about forty-three seconds after walking away from trying. *Mistake. Very big mistake.*

I watched her leave a few minutes ago. I saw her on the sidewalk with Ava, where they talked for a moment, then they hugged before going to Lulu's Ice Cream Shop across the street. It's less a whole shop and more of a walk-up, with a few small tables right out front. I glance over at them again through the window, seeing Drew dig through her purse. *Is she counting change to pay for their ice cream?*

"Hey, Hawk?" Will calls from the back office, pulling my attention in her direction.

I duck my head in while she reads something from the computer screen.

"Good news," she says. "The permits for expansion were approved on that space next door so we get to start next week. The contractor will be here later this week to discuss. The plan is to renovate most of the space before knocking down the dividing wall so we can continue to work the majority of the time."

I nod. I've had my eye on the vacant space next door for months. The bakery that previously occupied it closed about six months ago and it's been on the market ever since. I made my move as soon as they slapped a **REDUCED PRICE** notice on the window, taking it as a sign to pull the trigger. I have major plans. Plans that include an additional tattoo artist or two coming on board, among other things.

"You're getting that weird grin across your face again, man," she says.

I walk in and sit across from her, propping my feet up on the desk as I laugh and rub my hands together. "Yes, I know."

"It weirds me out." She furrows her eyebrows in mock horror.

She knows the only times I show any type of enthusiasm is when I'm talking about work or my future plans for it. I give her my most sinister grin and waggle my eyebrows, and she snorts. For as long as I can remember, she's always snorted while laughing. It's not obnoxiously loud, but it's definitely there. She hates it, but I don't. I find it endearing and uniquely my friend.

"What do you think of Drew?" she asks.

Ugh. Just when I thought I might not have to. "She seems fine." I shrug. Determined to change the subject, I continue with, "What are you doing tonight?"

"Just gonna finish up here then go home and cuddle my cat," she says.

"That's sad."

"I fucking know, right? I'm the single cat lady." She sighs, sagging further into her chair.

"Please don't get this sad on a Monday. Wait until at least

Thursday. The week will be almost over then," I encourage. For selfish reasons mostly. I can't have five days of Will sulking around this place. I'll go insane.

She folds her arms over her chest, jutting her bottom lip out at me. I roll my eyes, and then we proceed to have a stare-off. Such has been our relationship for the better part of our lives.

"Fine," she finally says. "So, what are we going to do about Ava?"

Ah, Christ. I can't escape it. "I'm sorry, what?"

"You heard me," she says.

"I did, but I don't know what you want me to say. We can't have a kid hanging around the tattoo shop every day," I say, throwing my hands up.

Will tilts her head at me. She does this when I'm being…well, me—Hawk Tanner. Sort of an asshole.

"Well, we have to think of something. We can't have her outside on a bench every day either," Will says.

"How is that our problem?" I ask.

"Hawk Anthony Tanner!" She snaps.

"You did fucking not. You did fucking not just middle name me, Willette Susan Archer."

"You know damn well we take care of our own. As of today, Drew's our own. And that includes Ava. And do not *Susan* me," she says, her eyes burning bright. I'm the only one here who knows her middle name and exactly how much she loathes it.

I fold my arms over my chest, chewing on her words. *Okay, but what am I supposed to do? Pay for daycare? Do kids her age go to daycare?* "How old is Ava? Do you know?"

"Drew said she's eight," she says.

I stand from the desk and walk out of the office, processing this information as best as I can. *Renovations will be starting. Drew is one of us. Ava needs to not be on the bench. Okay, Hawk, think.*

Stupid Will. Can't she mind her own business?

No. The answer is no. She always sticks her nose into shit. Is always trying to help, always trying to make things better. It's one of the things I most admire and despise about her. Of course, why she has to drag me into her meddling the majority of the time is another thing entirely.

Why can't she figure it out? Why can't she just do whatever she wants me to do and leave me out of it?

Why is it becoming my problem?

I'm annoyed—again. My appointments are done for the day, so I clean up my area and look across the street. Drew and Ava are already gone. I think about Will's insistence and decide she's probably right. Sure, a tattoo shop is no place for a kid to be hanging out. But then again, neither is a bench outside of one. I grab my stuff and head out the back and upstairs to grab Raven. She needs a good long walk and so do I. Maybe it'll help clear up the fog in my mind.

I'm in and out after changing into basketball shorts and a V-neck T-shirt and putting a leash on Raven. The looks we get are one of my favorite parts of taking her out. I'm the big scary tattooed guy and she's the ferocious black pitbull. People wind around us like water around a rock on the paths in the park, but I don't mind. I like my space. I'm content letting them think we'll both rip their faces off if they're not careful.

"Hawk!"

A voice from my not-so-distant past comes calling and I wonder if I can outrun it right here right now in the park.

I turn to see how far away she is. *Too fucking close.* That's all that really matters.

She stomps her feet right up to me and I can hear Raven growling in the back of her throat.

"Hey, Nina," I say.

Regret. So much regret wrapped up in one redhead.

SHAKE THE FROST

DREW

Will presses my first paycheck into my hand on Friday morning and I'm so happy, there may even be tears forming in the corners of my eyes. I try to hold them back, keep them from falling. I delicately grip the envelope in my hand. It's the first one I've earned on my own in years. I nod and turn to leave.

"Good job this week," she says.

"Thank you—really," I say, turning back toward her.

"Hawk won't say it, but he thinks you're doing a good job too," she assures.

I nod again and before the tears actually start to fall, I make a beeline for the bathroom, where I quickly shut the door behind me. I stand in front of the sink and sniffle, wiping at the corners of my eyes. Ripping the envelope open, I pray it's enough for some essentials and to save for the bills.

On one hand, I'm happy I'm being paid weekly. On the other hand, that means smaller sums of money. I look at the amount and start doing the math. *This can't be right.* This is more than what it should be. *I think? Isn't it?* I look at the line items and there's a gratuity line. *Gratuity?*

I walk back out and into the office.

"Will, what's this?" I ask.

"Oh, that's not typical of tattoo shops, but it's something Hawk and I decided on. The artists are tipped so we try to average it, do some math, and tip you out sort of like a hostess at a restaurant, if that makes sense?"

"Oh, okay," I say, nodding and trying to follow along.

"The guys are cool with it. Plus, it helps make up for the fact that we don't offer insurance or anything. At least, not yet," she says.

"Okay, great. Thanks," I say, not wanting to take up too much of her time. I start to back out of the office, near tears all over again because how fucking generous of them. This place is amazing.

"Hey, wait. What are you doing tonight?" Will asks.

"Um, nothing. I'll just be home with Ava."

"Do you want to get a drink? Hang out maybe?"

"I can't. I have Ava," I say, my eyes moving to the floor.

"That's okay. I can just come to your place?" she offers.

I smile because the thought of making a friend is nice. I could really use at least one. "That would be great."

"Awesome. How's eight?"

"Works for me," I tell her.

I head toward the front to resume my place at the counter, pausing to stuff the envelope in my purse that's hanging on the coat rack. As I pass the artists' booths, I look around to see what everyone's working on, because I actually enjoy that part of the job.

Hanson is stenciling a rather simple flash onto a girl's shoulder. Avery—or, errr... *Spider*—is tattooing a large piece on a guy's back. And Hawk is working on the thigh of a woman. She's staring at him like he's covered in jewels and I stifle a laugh. Come to think of it, all the women that come into the shop look at him like that. Not that I blame them. *I think it's the jaw. But I already said that.*

"Hey, Drew?" Hawk calls for me just as I'm past his booth and I take a few steps back.

"Yes?" I reply, a little taken aback that he's calling for me, especially mid-appointment.

He hasn't really attempted to speak to me since the papers-on-the-floor debacle. I chalked that awkward moment up to temporary insanity on his part. Since then, he's resumed his quiet demeanor of flexing the aforementioned jaw, drawing in his sketchbook, and listening to music as often as he can. I think the music is a means to avoid people, but I can't say with certainty.

"I've been thinking about Ava," he says, and this startles me. It also kind of weirds me out but I wait for it to make sense before I deck him.

"Okay..." I say, hesitantly.

"Will told me she doesn't want her to sit out back anymore so if you want, I have an alternative. If you're okay with it," he says.

I look to the front lobby and then the back office, wondering if anyone else is hearing this because it sounds so strange to me. "Okay. What is it?"

"Let's talk after I finish up here," he says.

I nod to him and walk to the front, where I pull up the electronic calendar and sneak a look at the client he's working on. Leanna is getting a dolphin scene on her thigh.

I straighten all the magazines in the front lobby and then organize the artists' portfolios. I run my fingers over the front of Hawk's and slowly open to a random page where there are photographs of a woman's back. Brightly colored flowers are beautifully inked all the way down her spine.

I flip to the next page. A man's chest is proudly displayed, waves crashing around Poseidon holding a trident and other nautical paraphernalia. *Wow.* I guess if I do want a tattoo, choosing Hawk would be a good choice. His work is stunning.

I hear the tattoo machines stop and realize Leanna is done getting her dolphins. So I walk back to the front desk to process the payment for her, while Hawk stays in his booth to clean up.

"Can you give this to him?" she asks. She slides me a generous tip—several twenty-dollar bills, with what appears to be her phone number written on a piece of paper on top.

"Um, sure," I say.

Leanna beams and scurries out the front door, her mostly bare thigh bandaged beneath her shorts.

I walk back to Hawk's booth and hold out what she left behind. "Um, she left this for you," I say, barely able to get the words out.

"If it's her number, I don't want it," he says, his back still to me as he continues to clean his workspace.

"Well, it's not just her number," I add.

"Put her tip in the cash box," he says.

I look down at what is easily a hundred-dollar tip if not more, my eyes growing wide.

He finally turns to see me, as if he realizes how awkward I feel. "Actually just keep it. Consider it payment for the pain and suffering she put you through with this awkward request." With that, he smirks.

Holy shit, ladies and gentlemen. That was a smirk. Almost a whole ass smile. A fucking facial expression. *He is alive!*

"I'll just put it in the cash box," I say.

"Suit yourself," he says. "Oh, wait, about Ava. Will is worried about her being out there. So, uh, follow me." He points to the back door of the shop and we walk out onto the patio. Then he turns to the stairs at our right and points up. When we get to the top, he unlocks the door and opens it slowly, motioning for me to go inside.

"This is my place," he says behind me, still standing near the door.

I look around, and it's not what I expected at all. Light filters in through tall windows. The furniture is light and comfortable looking. The outer walls are all exposed brick, and the hardwood floors are accented with plush rugs. What I can see of the kitchen is modern and light as well. White granite countertops and dark cabinets, with stainless steel appliances.

Movement catches my eye and before I know it, a big black pitbull is standing at my feet wagging its whole butt. Its whole face is smiling up at me and I kneel to pet it.

"That's my girl, Raven," he says.

"Hi, Raven," I say in my best baby dog voice. Raven rewards my efforts with several dog kisses across my cheek.

"Wow, she usually isn't so friendly," Hawk says.

I look up to see him rubbing the back of his neck, staring down at my encounter with Raven.

"Maybe she just knows how much I love John Wick," I say, giggling as Raven continues to lick me.

"Well, anyway, Ava could come up here if you want. I mean, if you're okay with it. Until you get off," Hawk says. He shifts uncomfortably and shoves his left hand in his pocket.

"I couldn't ask that of you," I start.

"You're not asking, I'm offering," he says plainly.

"You're sure?" I ask.

"She can keep Raven company, unless she's afraid of dogs? And she'll be more comfortable up here."

"All right, we can try it out if it's okay," I say. "But if it becomes too much or a bother in any way, she doesn't have to."

He nods and turns toward the door. "All right, yeah. We can bring her up today and show her before you guys leave. You can stay with her for a few just to kind of get her used to it then take off work early. She can start coming up here Monday," he says.

I stand there, pulling my fallen jaw up until my lips meet. I think this is what shock feels like.

I would have sworn to anyone five days ago that Hawk didn't have a heart.

But now...

Maybe there is something knocking around in the walls of that ribcage. Maybe it's small, maybe it's a little frozen. But I think it just might be in there—thawing.

THE CUPID SHUFFLE
DREW

I t occurred to me while I was in the store trying to pick wine, that I don't really know a lot about Will. For example, what kind of wine she drinks. Or the food she might eat. *Is she a vegetarian? One of those vegan people?* You can't very well invite someone over to your house and only have peanut butter and jelly and some nearly black bananas in your kitchen.

So when I got off work early, courtesy of Hawk, I took advantage by stopping at the market on the way home and grabbing several items. Then, I ran home as quickly as I could to straighten up the apartment and put away all the groceries. I also concluded that being in sweatpants would be all right, considering this is a girls' night of staying in and likely vegging out.

Which brings me to now—fifteen minutes before she's supposed to be here, standing at my counter in sweatpants and a tank top, holding the cheapest bottles of both red and white wine I could find and staring down at a makeshift charcuterie board I created by ripping open a couple of Lunchables and adding fruit. It felt like a brilliant idea at the time, but now I feel like an idiot and I'm cussing under my breath about my life decisions in general.

Granted, my check was more than I expected. And after Hawk and I showed Ava the apartment and she met Raven, he still insisted I keep that tip. But I need to save as much as I can for bills and things needed for the apartment. Not to mention, I would like to be able to buy some new clothes at some point.

I twist to look at the mason jar on top of the fridge. I deposited most of my check into my account, some into my savings, and then the cash went straight into the jar—*a rainy day fund*. It's one of the only pieces of advice I remember getting from my parents when they were still alive.

A knock at the door interrupts my thoughts and I check my watch, realizing I've been standing here rearranging this plate of miniature meats and cheeses longer than I thought.

I pass by Ava, who's sprawled out on the living room floor, feet kicking through the air, drawing what appears to be a house with people in front of it. Not stick people. No, not Ava. For reasons unknown to me, Ava is actually quite talented. And she doesn't get it from me or her father.

I unlock the deadbolt and chain to a very relaxed and cheerful Will, who's holding up a bottle of white wine. *White wine. Commit that to memory, Drew.* I'm also happy to see she's wearing leggings and a sweatshirt that hangs off one shoulder.

"Hey, girl," she says.

She's only called me by my first name this week, so the friendly greeting throws me off for a moment, but it feels nice. When I moved, I left what few friends I had behind too. Making a few new ones is right up there with wanting to be able to afford pants that aren't slacks.

"Hi. Come on in," I say. "The place isn't much but it's home, for now."

She walks in and looks around. "Looks fine to me. Except, you need some art on the walls for sure. But with this one here, I'm sure you'll have that problem solved in no time." She says this as she's looking down at Ava and I smile. She's right about that.

If I let Ava have her way, she would cover the entire apartment with pictures. Which, come to think of it, wouldn't be the worst idea. Certainly better than some of the stains and scuffs adorning them now.

"Let's go get some glasses," I say, leading Will into the kitchen.

I set the wine down on the counter as I stretch and reach, trying to find two decent glasses in the cabinet. There's nothing close to resembling a wine glass, so I grab two coffee mugs instead.

"Ah, perfect," she says, laughing. "I prefer my wine holder to come with a handle anyway."

"You're not a vegan, are you?" I ask.

"God, no." She laughs. "Why do you ask?"

I point to the plate of snacks and let it answer the question for me.

Without hesitation, Will stacks a cracker, what I think is a ham slice, and a piece of yellow cheese, then shoves it into her mouth. "I freaking love snacks," she declares.

I smile at myself, satisfied with my work, and return to my task of pouring the wine.

As I hand her a mug that says **CAFFEINE ADDICT** she says,

"So, what's your story? I mean, I know the short version, but what's the long one?"

I walk over to the kitchen table and sit on the stool, motioning for her to join me. She follows, mug and broke-girl charcuterie board in hand, sitting in the one good chair across from me. I figure if I want to make friends, I'll have to spill the sordid details of my past eventually. Will feels good and trustworthy enough to me for this.

"I haven't been a single mom very long," I admit, more like a confession, lowering my voice so Ava can't hear.

Will leans in, picking up on this. "What happened?"

"Her father, Curtis, filed for divorce without even really discussing it with me." I take a sip of my wine before I continue. "Did I mention he's an attorney?"

Will's eyes grow wide with worry. Or maybe it's shock. I'm not really sure. I wouldn't be surprised if it were both. "Does he live close?" she asks.

"No, and that's the way I want it," I say. "He told me he didn't love me anymore and that's fine. But when he told me he didn't want anything to do with Ava, I nearly lost it."

"Jesus, what a fuck." Will quickly covers her mouth, glancing into the living room toward Ava.

I laugh and nod in agreement. "Yeah, he is a fuck."

"Well, you're part of the Bird's Eye family now," she says.

"About that..." I start. "I understand you're the reason Ava doesn't have to wait on the bench anymore. I really appreciate that."

"All I did was tell Hawk we needed to figure something out," she says, raising her hands in innocence. "The rest was his idea."

What. The. Actual. Fuck?

"Really?" I ask, not trying to hide the shock in my expression.

"Yep." She nods and sips her wine. Then, she reaches for a grape and pops it into her mouth while I let this new information roll around in my head.

"I thought he hated me." I laugh.

Will's head jerks up and she stares, bewildered. "What on earth would give you that impression? Do we know the same Hawk?

"Well, he's not exactly the friendliest. And he barely talks to me," I say.

"That's just Hawk. Believe it or not, he's talked to you more in the past week than he spoke to Hanson in the first three months he worked here."

Wow. That's a whole lot of not talking. "What's his deal? Why is he like that?"

Will shrugs. "I've known the guy since we were in fourth grade. And honestly, I don't know if he's ever *not* been like that."

I think about this as I stack a cracker with meat and cheese. I bite into it just as she makes her next statement.

"He's single, you know." She smirks.

I begin to choke, feeling a chunk of the tiny ham slice flip flopping in my throat. Bits of cracker spew from my mouth as Will laughs. She's clearly not too concerned with my safety. *Didn't someone famous die by choking to death on a ham sandwich? Or was that fake news?* Either way, it's believable for a reason.

I finally stop coughing long enough to take a few sips of my wine and look over at Will, who is positively radiant—her chin perched on the back of her hand, elbow propped on the table. She stares at me expectantly.

"Yeah, I don't think that would work. Or be a good idea. Or work. Or be something he'd be interested in," I ramble.

"Ah ha!" she says rather enthusiastically.

I throw my head back at her apparent discovery and wait, shifting my eyes left to right.

"But you didn't say you weren't interested," she says.

I swallow hard. *Because, what?* "No, I…I've never dated anyone like Hawk."

"Doesn't mean you can't," she says. She seems so matter of fact about it.

"Something tells me he doesn't date women like me either," I say confidently.

"Women like…beautiful women? Independent women? Smart women?" she muses, waving her hand through the air in an exaggerated gesture as if she's trying to remind me about myself.

I feel my cheeks warm and know they're flushed pink under the weight of her words. "No. I mean single mothers. Mothers in general. With kids. Women who own more slacks than jeans. Divorcées."

Will swirls the wine in her mug and shoots the last bit back before standing and walking to the counter for more. "Yeah, maybe he's never dated someone like that. But that's not who you are. If anything, those things just solidify the fact that you're totally badass. Minus the slacks thing. We should really go shopping. That's just not normal," she says, laughing.

I laugh too and then change the subject, asking her about the plans for expansion.

I need time to chew on her compliments and forget about her ridiculous suggestion.

She would make the worst Cupid.

AN EPIC OF TIME WASTED
HAWK

Ever since Will told me she was going to Drew's house to hang out tonight, I haven't been able to stop thinking about it. *What are they doing, anyway? What are they talking about? Where does Drew even live?*

I shoot Will a quick text and put my phone down, trying to concentrate on the fact that, despite not wanting to be here, Nina has dragged me to a bar down the street from the shop. She probably thinks we're getting back together but honestly, I'm just trying to hang in there long enough to see if I can convince her to give me Sadie—the other pitbull we had when we lived together.

The agreement when we split was that she'd take Sadie and I'd take Raven. I didn't like it then and I don't like it now. She doesn't give a shit about Sadie; she took her to hurt me. I've regretted agreeing to it ever since. I should've fought for her.

So here I sit, watching her twirl one of her bright red extensions between her fingers. For the record, I don't give a fuck if a woman wears extensions. But Nina's look like shit and they aren't the same color as the rest of her hair and despite trying to subtly tell her the entire time we were together, she didn't fix it.

Nina's giving me that look she always gave me when she thought we were going to fuck, but that's not going to happen.

"Do you want to get some food?" I ask.

She lazily peers down at the menu and tilts her head like she's having a hard time reading it or some shit. It's fucking bar food. It's not hard to read F-R-I-E-S and N-A-C-H-O-S.

"Maybe some mozzarella sticks," she says.

I hold my hand up in the air to signal the waitress in the corner. "How's Sadie?" I ask Nina, and she smirks. Because she knows.

"Oh, she's good. She misses her daddy though," she says. "And the feeling is mutual."

Fucking. Yuck.

"I miss her too," I say, skipping right over the pedophile-infused kink I still can't seem to get on board with. I tried—I really did. It's just not my thing.

She huffs, and this is her way of letting me know she noticed I skipped over saying I missed her.

I order the food, taking a big gulp of my vodka afterward as I sit back in my chair. I try to look at Nina again with fresh eyes. A renewed sense of...*I don't know? Less judgment?* Her fake red hair still annoys me but it's just hair. I can get over that. It looks like she stopped with the spray tanning, thank god.

I know what you're thinking: Why? Why, Hawk?

She reaches across the table and strokes my arm with her long acrylic nails.

I. Don't. Fucking. Know. Okay? I don't know. I was drunk at a friend's party. We hooked up. We hooked up again. One thing led to another and then we were living together and getting dogs. Once we had the dogs I couldn't leave, because I loved the dogs. I never loved Nina. Just the dogs. I know that doesn't make me a swell guy, but shit happens.

The back of my neck itches and I try not to pull my arm away from her touch to rub it because she'll huff again and I'll get nowhere. But then my phone buzzes on the table and thankfully she gets distracted by her own phone, so I take the opportunity to pick mine up.

Will: Yep, made it safe and sound. Please tell me you're not with Nina?

Me: I'm just trying to get Sadie.

Will: Don't sleep with her for a dog.

Me: I would do a lot of things for a dog.

Will: Dude.

Me: Dude.

Me: Anyways. What are you guys even doing?

"And here are your mozzarella sticks and onion rings," the waitress says, setting the plates down on the table between us and drawing our attention from our phones, which Nina and I place down almost in unison to focus on the food.

I lay a napkin over my lap and reach for an onion ring.

"Do you think if I came by this week, you could finish this?" Nina asks, pulling the edge of her shirt over to show me the half-finished weird paw print design on her right tit.

I cringe inwardly, biting down on the onion ring to keep from saying something I'll regret. "Yeah, sure." I pick my phone back up to look at my calendar and see a notification from Will. I swipe past it to open up the week in question. "I don't have anything going on Wednesday."

"That works for me. What time?" she asks.

"Ten? First one of the day?" I ask.

"Perfect," she says, a smile spreading across her lips.

Her dark purple lipstick is partially smeared off onto the cheese she's eating out of her mozzarella stick and it's pretty gross, but if I don't make direct eye contact I won't get what I came for. I sort of have to treat her whole face like an eclipse and stare near the top of her head instead.

"Great." I type her name into the calendar on my phone so it syncs to the calendar at work and no one books me.

Then I remember Will's notification and flip to my texts. I click on Will's name and my screen fills with a photo. Will and Drew are sitting on an ugly green couch, their pink cheeks pressed against each other's. They appear to be mid-laugh, and if I know Will—and I do—they're a little tipsy. Probably on white wine.

I study Drew's face, her features soft, relaxed. She's at ease, her guard down. She doesn't look like this at work.

"Hello?" Nina's voice cuts through my thoughts like one of those annoying South Park voices.

"Yeah, what?" I ask, giving her my attention.

"Are you even listening?"

"Sorry, what were you saying?" I ask.

She huffs again. *Not good.* I'm one huff away from never seeing Sadie again. "I was saying maybe I could come over Wednesday after work? Bring Sadie? But if you're too distracted…"

"No, I'm not. That sounds good. Really," I say, the excitement in my voice palpable again because it's actually real. Seeing Sadie is the *only* reason I'm here.

"Okay, then. It's a date." She smirks, twirling her goddamn extension again.

I want to throw my onion rings up, but I press my lips into a line and manage a stiff nod.

She turns her attention back to sipping the tall monstrosity of a drink she ordered. It's blue, with fruit floating in it. She sucks on the straw while giving me her best fuck-me eyes and I swallow hard to keep the onion rings at bay once more. She crams half a cheese stick in her mouth, and I swallow the rest of the vodka in my glass, calculating just exactly how long I'll need to keep her in my apartment to separate her from Sadie before kicking her out.

It's not dognapping if it's your dog, is it?

She has no ownership papers. *Yes, this could work.*

I slosh the vodka around in my mouth, trying to get rid of the onion taste because everything is making me feel sick now.

I keep my eyes down because I can't look up at Nina again. I just can't do it.

My phone dings again and I pull it into my lap, flipping up the screen to reveal another picture notification from Will. This is a candid shot of Drew. She's sitting on the opposite end of the couch, smiling, and it appears as if she were talking about something. Her eyes are lit up in that honey color I saw on her first day of work.

I have a sudden itch to sketch those eyes, use colored pencil to bring them to life.

"What are you smiling at?" Nina cuts into my thoughts again.

"Nothing," I say, snapping my phone shut before waving the waitress over for another vodka. Because I need another vodka if I'm going to be here any longer.

I'm still thinking of Drew's honey eyes. I'm still contemplating Sadie's dognapping. I keep my lips pressed into a straight line, trying to give Nina my best poker face.

I don't want to be doing this. I don't have time for this. But sacrifices must be made. I'm praying I don't have to sleep with her to make it happen because—and I say this with every ounce of bravery I can muster—I don't think I can get it up for her.

ELASTIC HEART
DREW

I bite into the most delicious chocolate cream donut and bless Will and her insistence on Monday morning donuts because *yeee-ummm*. She and I spent all weekend texting and even went shopping.

By last night, it hit me: *Holy shit, I've got a friend.* A real, actual friend.

When I say we went *shopping*, I mean Will showed me her favorite places to shop since I'm new to the area. To my relief, she prefers thrift shops over designer stores. I didn't mention my budget to her, but thrift is about all I can afford right now so it worked out perfectly. Somehow though, Will's choice in second-hand items weren't nearly as disappointing as my Aunt Penny's.

Perhaps bargain hunting has changed in the past thirty years. Perhaps Will just knows the right shops from the wrong ones. Either way, she showed me the ropes. Because admittedly, when I was the wife of a prominent attorney, I wasn't exactly well-versed.

Still, when I approached the register with the biggest stack of clothes I could carry, I started to get nervous about what it might cost. I had easily several hundred dollars' worth of stuff. But when the cashier told me my total—twenty-eight freaking dollars —I almost cried.

Which is why this Monday morning, I've dared to wear these awesome black skinny jeans with rips all the way up the thighs and this tank top that's shredded at the bottom. It's obviously not my typical style, but I'm embracing all the changes. I even have killer boots on. I feel fucking badass in this outfit.

I'm wiping chocolate from my lips when I hear the back door open, followed by the familiar scuff of boots.

"Hey, Hawk," I call. This is our cursory greeting. Nothing fancy.

His eyes are downcast but when he looks up at me, he stops his forward movement. His eyes skim over my boots and up my legs, lingering on my thighs and midsection before finally reaching my face.

"Did you fall in Will's closet?" he asks.

"No, these are mine." *Geez, can't the guy just give a compliment?*

He makes a *hmph* sound as he walks past me and into his booth, where he removes his jacket and sits down.

Well, that's that I guess. And Will thought we could date? Yeah right.

I turn my attention back to my donut and open the electronic calendar so it's ready to input requests for today. I skim over it to familiarize myself with what we have going on this week when I see a new entry. On Friday I distinctly remember Hawk's Wednesday being empty but now it's completely blocked out, and only with one name. *Nina.* I didn't put that in, so he must have done it himself over the weekend. *Strange.*

"Hey, Drew," Will says to me as she pours her third cup of coffee.

The girl does love her coffee. My **CAFFEINE ADDICT** mug was definitely appropriate for her and I consider bringing it in for her as a gift.

"What's up?" I ask.

"You went to college, right?" she asks.

"Uh, for like a year and a half," I admit. "I didn't finish." I can feel Hawk's eyes on us, as if he's listening, but I ignore the urge to turn toward him.

"I think I need your help with something if you don't mind," Will says.

"Sure." I pop the last bit of donut into my mouth and follow her into the office.

She shuts the door behind me—and she only shuts the door when shit is serious. She sits down at the desk and I follow her lead, crossing my legs, waiting for her to deliver some kind of bad news.

"You're good with numbers and stuff, right?" Will asks.

I blink a few times. "Well, before I dropped out of college, I took some accounting courses and stuff? Why?"

"So, with the expansion and running this shop, I've got just a little more than I can handle management wise. I was wondering if you'd be willing to help out with the books and other management duties?"

I hesitate. I don't know why I hesitate, but I do. Maybe because I don't want to let her down.

"Of course, that means you'd be paid more," she adds. "And Hawk and I have discussed a permanent Assistant Manager position after the expansion is complete."

"I'm in," I say quickly.

Will grins at me, seeming pleased with herself as she thrusts her fist through the air like she's won a prize. "Great! Later this week, I want to run through some project-related details and give you the contact information for several people involved. I'll walk you through the space next door too," she says.

I tell her I'm excited for the new responsibilities and leave the office feeling good. Really fucking good. So good in fact, I grab another donut on my way back to the front counter. I stop abruptly because Hawk is standing there, leaning over said counter. No one else is there, no customer to help. He's just hanging out in my space. I broaden my shoulders, hold my chin up, and approach.

"Why did you only go to college for a year and a half?" he asks bluntly. No easing in with Hawk. No small talk. He gets straight to the point.

"I got pregnant," I tell him.

His eyes grow wide and he blinks his shock away. He looks like he's trying to do calculus in his head.

"I'm twenty-seven and Ava is eight. I was nineteen," I say.

"What about her father?" he asks.

Wow, this guy...

"Curtis was twenty-one and stayed in school to finish his law degree." I shrug my shoulders. "When I dropped out, it made the most sense for me to focus on raising Ava and supporting Curtis while he finished so we could all have a good life."

Hawk's jaw flexes as he chews on this information. "Where is Curtis now?"

"I'm not really sure," I say. "Probably back in our old house or traveling. Far away from here is all I know for sure."

"He doesn't see Ava?" Hawk asks.

"No, he doesn't want to," I say, my voice shrinking a bit at the sting of memories.

Hawk straightens, and his hands bunch into fists at his sides. I watch the muscles from his forearms all the way up to his shoulders roll and tighten. His lips press into that signature line of his, and then he turns to walk away without saying another word.

"Oh, that reminds me," I say, halting him. "Well, not so much the stuff about Curtis, but Ava. I know we aren't supposed to have kids here, but she has a school day coming up where she's supposed to go to work with one of her parents. I told her she might not be able to come here, and it's okay if you say no, but I just thought—"

"It's fine," he interrupts.

"Really?" I ask, just to make sure I heard him correctly.

"Yeah, she can come in," he says. He walks back to his booth and sits down.

I stare at the back of his head for several minutes wondering what the fuck just happened because either Hawk had an aneurysm or maybe I did.

"Okay, she will be in on Friday with me!" I call to him.

He waves his hand through the air, a very noncommittal confirmation.

Well, damn. Hawk is definitely not heartless.

SHE'S OUT OF HER MIND
HAWK

The last fucking thing in the world I want to do today is tattoo my ex-girlfriend. I don't want to sit and cradle her tit in my hand while she eye fucks me. I don't want her breathing in my face. And I don't want to waste perfectly good tattoo ink on stupid paw prints. On the other hand, stabbing her with a needle over and over again would have its merits. Perhaps it'll even be therapeutic.

I check the clock as I pace back and forth in the stock room. Nina is supposed to be here any minute, and I just need a few moments to decompress and put on my game face. I roll my shoulders and neck. This needs to go well. I need to get Sadie.

You can do this, Hawk. Just one more time.

The stock room door flies open and Will appears. She crosses her arms over her chest and starts tapping her foot.

"What?" I ask.

"Why the fuck is Hurricane Nina in our lobby?" she asks.

This sort of thing is one of the reasons I'm relieved Will doesn't pay attention to the client calendar.

"She wants me to finish her tattoo," I say plainly.

"Since when the fuck and why the fuck?"

"Since the other night and so I can get Sadie," I snap.

Will rolls her eyes but ultimately relaxes her shoulders, understanding it's a necessary evil. She pats me on the shoulder. "You should've had both dogs from the beginning anyway."

"Don't I fucking know it," I say, running my hand down my face.

After several more minutes, I shake out the last bit of disgust I have for the situation and walk toward the door. "Let me get this over with," I say.

I approach the front counter, where I find Nina having a full-on discussion—with Drew—about her boob job, and I'm completely mortified. Like, I'm actually embarrassed for myself. *Is this really happening?*

"Let's go." I nod to Nina and she follows me back to my booth, where she's pawing at my forearm and leaning in too close.

Drew is looking at us and I want to die. Or throw Nina in a hole somewhere and forget I ever knew her. Nina sits down and I perch on my stool, slapping on my gloves, completely prepared to get straight to the business end of this.

"New girl seems nice," she says, smacking her gum.

Her fucking gum. One of us isn't going to survive this.

"Yeah, she's fine," I say, pouring ink into the small cups in front of me.

"You fuck her yet?" she asks.

"Jesus Christ, Nina." My tone is a hushed exclamation.

She laughs too loud with her mouth wide, and I can see the

gum in her mouth bobbing up and down as she snorts. "Relax, I was only kidding. She ain't exactly your type."

"What do you mean?" I ask.

"Are you kidding me? Look at her. She's just so plain."

So I do. I look at Drew. She's restocking the swag on the shelves and smiling at something Hanson said. She doesn't look plain. Not to me.

I like the way she brushes her blonde hair back over her shoulders, the way it bounces side to side when she walks. I like her skin—a pale, blank canvas. It doesn't stop me from wanting to drag a needle across it but maybe that's just a side effect of what I do. And any man alive can see she has a nice body. And her eyes. Honey colored prisms that dance in the light.

I snap my eyes back down to what I was doing before she notices. "Yeah, I guess you're right."

"I know you, Hawk," Nina says.

I don't have the heart to tell her that even though we were together for a year, she really doesn't. Not a single thing. She doesn't know I hate the sound of gum snapping and popping. She doesn't know that I hate her fake red hair. And she doesn't know that even though 80% of her wardrobe consists of skintight bodysuits like the one she has on now, I fucking hate them. Always have. Especially when they plunge all the way down to almost her belly button.

Now, don't get me wrong. I'm all for occasionally flaunting what you got. Showing off your body. Dressing sexy. It was mostly just the fact that Nina was the one doing it.

I press the needle to Nina's tit and she moans. *God.* Everything she does is so over the top. I have to mash the whole thing down with my hand and she arches her back, taking full advantage of the cheap moment. *Gross.*

"So, what time should I come over later?" she asks.

She just has to do it, doesn't she? "Six?" I suggest.

"Yeah, that works for me," she says, and I cringe. But then she adds, "Sadie can't wait to see her daddy."

And with that, I'm reminded why I'm putting up with this in the first place.

The rest of her tattoo appointment is filled with me trying to be nice but being mostly short when I answer her, and keeping my mind occupied with literally anything else I can think of. I occasionally find myself thinking of Drew.

She's not plain. Maybe Nina only thinks so because nothing about Nina is even close to simple or understated. Sure, if you put Nina next to anyone, including a rodeo clown, they'd look plain.

Drew is…*elegant. Subtle.* I don't know many women like her. At least, not in the world I'm used to. The world I live in, most women are like Nina. Or Rebecca, getting stupid dick tattoos. Will isn't so bad but she's like my sister so that's a hard no. Drew is different. Sweet but strong.

"Done," I say, putting a stop to my own thoughts and this sad tit tattoo.

Nina looks down, studying my work. "You're the best."

"Thanks," I mumble.

"What do I owe you?" she baits.

"Nothing."

She winks at me and squeezes my bicep. "I'll see you later."

With that, she walks out of my booth and through the front

lobby, past Drew, until she's out the front door and on the side-walk. I watch her put her obnoxiously large sunglasses on as she starts walking away.

It's almost over, Hawk. It's almost over.

THOSE KINDA NIGHTS
DREW

Ava is sitting at the kitchen table in the one good chair while I balance myself on the stool as we eat dinner. She tells me about her day at school and how she made a new friend named Jill.

I'm trying really hard to concentrate, but my mind is back on the events at work. The mysterious Nina and how disheveled her presence seemed to make Hawk before, during, and after her visit. He had barely recovered by the time I left and collected Ava from his apartment. I can't put my finger on it, but I'd venture to guess there's a lot more to that story. Not that I'd ever ask him.

Ava finishes telling me about her day and takes her plate to the sink, then bounces into the living room and down the hall to her bedroom. I stand to take my plate to the kitchen but her scream from the other room nearly causes me to drop the dish. I set my plate down on the counter and bound through the doorway.

With Ava, her horror movie squeal could mean anything from there's a spider crawling up her leg to we are out of toilet paper and she doesn't know what to do. The kid has a touch of theatrics in her blood to be sure, and like the artistic talent, I have no clue as to where she inherited it.

"What's wrong?" I ask, barreling into the bedroom to find her dumping the contents of her backpack onto the floor and sprawling them out.

"It's not here!" she cries.

"What's not here?" I ask.

"I must have left it at Hawk's apartment! We have to go get it, Mom!"

"Go get what?"

"My sketchbook!" Ava looks up at me with tears in her eyes.

"Can't we just get it tomorrow?" I ask, even though I already know the answer.

Her bottom lip starts to tremble and it's coming. "Please, Mom?"

I sigh and check my watch, seeing that it's quarter after six. If we hurry, we can make it back home by seven.

"Grab your jacket," I say, walking to go grab my own.

Let's just pray Hawk is in a better mood now than he was earlier.

———

WE MAKE THE WALK TO THE SHOP AND TAKE THE ALLEY around the building to the stairs leading up to Hawk's door. I hesitate at the bottom, one foot on the first step.

"Come on, Mom," Ava says, yanking at my hand.

We take the stairs together, hand in hand, and when we reach the top, Ava knocks before I can think better of this whole thing.

I hear noise inside. "Maybe he's busy," I say.

"Let's just wait one minute," Ava begs.

Before I can protest, the door swings open, but Hawk isn't the one who's opened it.

Nina—the woman from the shop earlier today—is standing in front of us, her long bright red hair falling over her plunging neckline. "Can I help you?" she asks.

Before I can say anything, Ava's innocence speaks. "I'm Ava," she says to Nina. "I left my sketchbook here earlier."

Nina looks at Ava then me and back at Ava.

Then I interject. "She waits here after school until I get off work," I say, trying my best to explain the situation.

Nina bends down to Ava and studies her like she's never seen a child before. "Well, why don't you go find it? Don't worry, Sadie won't hurt you."

Who the hell is Sadie?

I stand awkwardly in the door for several seconds until Nina finally waves me in.

"Do you want to come in and help her look?" she asks.

I nod before stepping into Hawk's apartment, realizing my daughter has spent more time here than I have. I watch Raven greet Ava and lick her face. Sadie, who must be the other dog, sniffs Ava's hands and then licks her, too. I look around but Hawk isn't anywhere in sight.

Ava starts picking up all the cushions on the couch. She was probably sitting on it and the sketchbook slid down into a crevice. It wouldn't be the first time, and likely not the last.

"So, how long have you been working at the shop?" Nina asks, interrupting my thoughts.

"This is only my second week," I say.

"Awfully nice of Hawk to let Anna up here while you work," she says, making an annoying snapping sound with her gum.

"Her name is Ava," I say sternly.

"Oh right, sorry," she says.

I get the impression that she isn't but I let it go. I turn my attention back to Ava, who's now on her hands and knees looking underneath the couch. She's not having any luck finding the sketchbook, which isn't good. I look around on the floor and on the chair closest to me when I hear noise come from the hall to my right.

"Who was there?" Hawk's voice cuts through the silence and I turn to see a shirtless Hawk standing at the entrance of the hallway.

Jesus. Goddamn. Forgive me, Father. Christ. My eyes cannot tear away from his tattooed torso. Ink covers nearly all of it. From the elastic edge of his boxer briefs all the way up to his throat and around the sides of his ribs. He's decorated. His body is a temple. Adorned.

He quickly covers himself with the T-shirt in his hands, clearly not expecting to see me or Ava in his living room at this moment in time. This very awkward moment in time when I am essentially sexually assaulting him with my eyes.

"God, I'm sorry. Ava left something here and we just came back to get it. God, I'm sorry," I say, half-running across the room and grabbing Ava by the hand. She's yelling protests and flailing.

"But, Mom—"

"We'll get it tomorrow. It's fine," I say, rushing out the door before anyone can say anything else.

I. Am. An. Idiot. That was a terrible idea. Of course he could and would have company in the evenings. *God, did we just interrupt a booty call? Is that what people call them? A date? Ew. That woman?* It's not like I know Hawk well, but I thought he'd at least date someone...different than that. Someone interesting or fun. Like Will. Or someone who at least doesn't make me want to stab myself in the eye. No matter, it's none of my business.

We stop at the store on our way back to our apartment and I let Ava get a new sketchbook to soothe the itch until we find her other one. Hopefully we *can* find the damn thing. She'll be heartbroken if we don't. She keeps all her drawings, and that sketchbook was over half full. I don't understand the importance myself, but I do my best to understand that while I may not care, my daughter does. So, if it's important to her, I don't belittle it.

Once we're home, she opens the new sketchbook only halfexcited and starts drawing. I deflate on my ugly cactus couch, pinching the bridge of my nose and cursing myself for the entire evening's events that unfolded.

Colossal mistake. Never go to your boss's apartment after hours. Never. Ever. Maybe get his number in case of emergencies—like this. Check beforehand. *Be a fucking adult maybe, Drew.* My head is spinning. Mostly about half-naked Hawk, which is the worst or best part. I'm not sure. Then, as if this can't get any worse, there's a knock on my door. And considering I don't know anyone here outside of work, I hardly expect this to be good.

I push up from the couch, wondering if it's that old lady from across the hall, and peer through the peephole. *Shit. Not the old lady.*

I open the door to see Hawk at my threshold. "Um, hi," I say. Because I don't know what the hell else to say.

"I think Ava was looking for this," he says, holding up her sketchbook.

I immediately relax my shoulders and call for Ava.

She rounds the corner, lighting up upon seeing what's here. "Oh my god, you found it!" She grabs the book from his hand and cradles it against her chest like it's her most prized possession.

"You guys left in a hurry. I didn't get a chance to tell you I found it and put it up to give you," he says. He puts his hand in his pocket and looks at me.

I press my lips together and look at Ava, who's soaking up every word. Then she does the unthinkable. She hands me the sketchbook, turns back to Hawk, and wraps her arms around him.

"Thank you so much, Hawk!" she says, squeezing him in the biggest hug her tiny eight-year-old body can manage.

I watch Hawk's body stiffen at first. He looks at me again and I smile, crossing my arms over my chest. *Yep, you made a friend, buddy.*

His body softens then, and he wiggles his hands and arms free to hug her in return, awkwardly patting her on the back. "No problem, kid."

She releases her grip and takes the sketchbook from me, then disappears back into the apartment.

"Thank you for finding it and bringing it to her. But I could've just gotten it tomorrow. You didn't have to, um, leave your... plans," I say awkwardly.

"Yeah, about that," he says. "We should talk."

HARD TO CONCENTRATE
DREW

"Would you like to come in?" I ask, swallowing hard, suddenly nervous about the idea of Hawk in my apartment, my personal space.

He nods, stepping past me as I close the door behind him. Hawk hovers at the edge of my living room, clearly uncomfortable and possibly unsure what to do.

"Would you like something to drink?" I ask, my ingrained hostess manners rearing their awkward head.

"No, I'm okay, thank you," he says.

I move past him toward the couch, sitting and gesturing for him to do the same.

He steps forward and slowly slides down onto the corner of the sofa, quite possibly as far away from me as he can manage while still being on the couch. "So, listen," he says. "I don't want you to think I was randomly hooking up with someone from the shop. Or that I'm hooking up with Nina at all."

"I mean, it's really none of my business," I say. "You don't owe me an explanation."

"No, this is important," he says, edging forward a hair. "Nina is my ex-girlfriend. And she's had my other dog, Sadie, since we broke up. I've been trying to play nice for as long as I can to get her back. I was only shirtless because she spilled something on me and I went to change."

Ohhhhh. Okay. I mean, I've seen his love for Raven, and I imagine he has that same love for Sadie, so I understand his motives. I nod for him to continue.

"She came by the shop earlier to get tattooed and insisted on coming over tonight. I agreed only with the intention of getting my dog back. I am not even remotely interested in getting back together with her," he says.

"Oh," I say. "Well, did you get her back?"

"Yes," he says. "Thank fuck. Because now I don't ever have to see her again."

I can't help myself as I start to laugh at his clear disgust with Nina. "Well, that's good then."

"Yeah, definitely," he says.

A few awkward moments go by, and I use them to wonder why he felt compelled to share any of this with me in the first place. He could have easily seen me tomorrow, or partially explained it.

"You came all this way just to tell me that?" I ask.

Hawk rubs the back of his neck, his eyes darting from my eyes, then down and back up again. "Uh, well, yeah." His hand moves from his neck toward me, like maybe he's going to touch me, but then he recoils. "I'm glad you work at the shop, and I really respect you. I just didn't want you thinking negatively of me."

"I like working at the shop too," I say. "And I respect you. I don't think bad of you." I swallow hard, acutely aware of his closeness.

"Good," he says, nodding. "Oh, and about Friday. Everything is set. I told the guys Ava is coming. They'll be on their best behavior."

"Oh, you didn't have to—"

"Don't worry about it." He cracks the smallest smile. I think it's meant to comfort me, but he smiles so rarely I feel like it's a gift.

"Well, okay. Great," I say.

"I should go," he says. "I'll um, see you in the morning."

"Thank you again for bringing her sketchpad over," I say, standing to walk him out.

Hawk nods and heads toward the door. As he steps into the hall, he turns, giving me one last hint of a smile, then disappears down the stairwell.

I close and lock the door, breathing a heavy sigh of relief. I shut my eyes for a moment to gather my composure. To try to figure out what the hell just transpired. *That was weird, right?* Maybe I'll ask Will about his behavior and if this is typical of him.

After I help Ava come up with ideas for some questions to ask my coworkers when she comes with me to work Friday, I help her into bed and tuck her in.

"Mom?" Ava asks.

"Yeah, baby?" I whisper.

"Do you think Hawk is nice?"

"Yeah, I think he is," I say.

"Do you think he's friendly?" she asks.

"Sure." I pull her blankets up under her chin, making sure she's snuggled in.

"Do you think he's handsome?" She giggles.

Oh dear. "I haven't really thought about it," I say, lying between my teeth because there's no way I am having this conversation with her now or possibly ever. And I sure as hell am not going to tell her that ever since I saw him shirtless, the image is burned into my retinas forever and I'll go to my grave being okay with that.

"I think he's handsome," she says, waggling her eyebrows at me.

"Ava Elaine," I say, half-laughing myself. "Goodnight. Go to bed, silly."

I shut the door to her bedroom and shake my head. She's crazy.

I'm surprised she'd even ask me that line of questions. Although, if I'm being honest, departing from her father hurt her pretty bad. She also saw how much it hurt me. I think in her mind, there's no way he's coming back. So maybe she's resolved to find me someone new. I can't express how much I hate this for her.

I rifle through my closet, trying to decide what to wear to work tomorrow before settling on some cutoff shorts. I saw Will wearing them, so I assume they're not against the dress policy. Actually, come to think of it, I'm not even sure there is a dress code of any kind. I'm guessing as long as we don't come in with our nipples showing, we're in the clear.

After my shower, I sit on the edge of the ugly green couch, rubbing my temples, thoughts swirling a tad violently in my head. They bounce between Hawk's tattooed chest, to liking and needing my job way too much to jeopardize it, to wondering if I will actually date again anytime soon. Between work and Ava, it's not as if I have a ton of free time.

The wounds left behind by Curtis are deep, and still very fresh. I'd hate to jump into something too soon and have it all backfire. Leave it to Ava's silly remarks to have me contemplating all my future decisions. *That kid.*

As I lie down on the lumpy ass couch, I begin to calculate exactly how long it'll take to fill my fridge jar with enough extra money to buy myself a proper bed. The answer is not soon enough. Too many more nights on this thing, and I'm going to give myself permanent back damage.

Despite everything, I still fall asleep to images of Hawk's skin, the swirling black ink wrapped around his body like vines. I imagine the expanse of his back, perfectly sculpted and adorned.

I can't stop myself from wondering what a man like him would look like naked, perfect and painfully beautiful.

TRIED TO BE NICE
HAWK

I couldn't tell you what possessed me to beg Nina for Sadie moments after Drew and Ava left. I literally clasped my hands together and offered her money. Which she gladly accepted in exchange for my dog. If I had known all she wanted was money, I would have offered it a long ass time ago. A thousand dollars and ten minutes later, Nina was gone, and I was running toward Drew's apartment after getting the address from Will at record speed.

I couldn't tell you why it was so important to me to set the record straight. To show up on her door unannounced like a psycho. But I did. I had to.

I also couldn't tell you why after Drew left work today, I pulled everyone into the office for a staff meeting to remind them that Ava would be here all day tomorrow and that everyone was to be on their best behavior. And that meant no cussing or inappropriate jokes. This was mostly directed toward Avery and Hanson.

I made it clear that no one was to be vulgar, and that everyone was to treat Ava like a goddamn princess and make this the best *Go to Work with Your Parent Day* any kid has ever had or I would personally murder them myself.

Why was that important to me? I don't know. I don't fucking know. Maybe it had something to do with the fucking cutoff shorts Drew wore today. Maybe it's just because that kid doesn't have a father anymore. She couldn't even choose to go to work with him if she wanted. So I want to make sure this workday thing is the best it possibly can be. For her.

———

I MADE SURE TO ARRIVE TO THE SHOP EARLY THIS morning, which is pretty unheard of for a typical Friday. Now, I'm standing here in my booth, cutting out temporary tattoos of fairies and other girly shit so I can show Ava what we do here. Well, sort of anyway. *God. What is happening to me?*

I hear the bell over the front door ding and look up to see Ava and Drew enter. Ava is all smiles, clearly excited to be here instead of at school. She waves at me and I wave back, trying my best to be less...me.

"Hi, Hawk," she says, approaching me.

I walk out of my booth and toward them. "Hello, ladies," I say.

"Ava is all ready. She's prepared a bunch of questions to ask everyone," Drew says, smiling down at Ava and stroking her hair.

"Well, the guys will be in any minute," I say to Drew. Then I turn my attention to Ava. "But first, I want to give you something. If that's okay?"

I watch Ava look up at her mom like maybe she needs permission to receive a gift from me, but Drew just nods.

I reach over the counter and grab the small gift bag with the items I bought after leaving their apartment and hand it to Ava.

"What is it?" she says excitedly.

"Just a little something for a little artist." I shrug.

She rips open the bag and pulls out a brand new sketchbook —but not the kind she's used to. This one has thicker pages and better texture for sketching. Then she pulls out the pencil kit and looks at it curiously.

"I noticed you were using the wrong kind of pencil," I say.

"Wrong kind?" she asks.

As I suspected, she doesn't know there's more than one kind of pencil. "I'll show you." I open the pencil box and point. "These pencils have softer lead, so the lines will be thicker and have more texture. These pencils have harder lead, so the lines are thinner, better for drawing initial lines and details."

I pull out my own sketchbook and flip to a blank page, demonstrating the difference. "These tools are for blending." I rub the point over where I've made lines and smooth out the marks, watching Ava's eyes light up.

She seems to be absorbing everything, fully invested in the tutorial. "Wow! These are amazing! Thank you so much, Hawk!" she says.

Then, for a second time this week, she reaches over to hug me. This time she hugs my neck, because I'm crouched down and she can reach it.

I pat her back again. "No problem, kid."

She tucks her new pencils and sketchbook into the backpack

she brought and gets out her notebook, apparently prepared for the business part of the day.

As I watch her flip through the pages of her notebook, I notice Drew watching me. I realize she's probably been watching the whole time, and her eyes are a little glossy.

"Okay," Ava cuts in. "I'm ready."

"Great, because I'm first, *princesa*." Hanson's voice echoes from the back hall, his Brazilian roots all over his preferred endearment. He reaches us a few moments later, wearing a crown. "Oh, and this one is for you!" he exclaims, presenting a tiara to Ava. "I'm Hanson, by the way. It's a pleasure to meet you."

"Um, I'm a little too old for crowns," Ava says. "But thank you, anyway."

I laugh. I actually laugh out loud. So loud they all look at me like I've grown a second head. But that shit was funny. I just watched Hanson get burned by an eight-year-old girl. She might be my new favorite person.

"Oh," Hanson says. "No problem." He deflates faster than a popped balloon.

"I'll wear it," Drew offers.

"No, it's okay. I'll wear it," Ava says. She walks over to Hanson and takes the tiara from him, then places it on her head. "It's great, Mr. Hanson. Thank you."

"Oh, it's just Hanson," he says.

Ava's quiet for a few seconds. "Okay. Are you ready, then?" she asks him.

I swear, this kid is the best. I look at Drew, who's facepalming, but I give her a look that hopefully conveys it's totally fine.

"Ava, I'll be over here if you need me," Drew says, but Ava is way too into giving Hanson shit to care about anything else.

I turn back to my booth but feel a hand on the back of my arm. I look over my shoulder and come face to face with Drew.

"Thank you for this. For everything, really," she says.

"Don't worry about it," I say, shrugging my shoulders.

"No, I'm serious. I really appreciate you guys going out of your way for her today," Drew says.

I look at Ava, and I can't be sure but I think I'm smiling. "Can I show you guys something tomorrow?"

"Tomorrow?" she repeats.

"Yeah, it's somewhere I think Ava will like," I say, fully using Ava to my advantage in persuading Drew to agree.

"Okay, sure," Drew says, nodding her head.

I nod before turning back to my booth, already devising a plan for tomorrow.

While I work, I listen to Ava talk to Hanson, then Avery. She won't call him Spider either because even someone her age knows it's a fucking dumb nickname.

Will explains to Ava what her job here entails, then shows her the office and the back stockroom. She gives Ava a Bird's Eye T-shirt and some stickers for her and her friends. Well, the age-appropriate ones, anyway.

Ava sits with her mom for a little while, watching what she does and helping answer a couple of calls.

Then it's my turn. I purposely asked Ava to interview me last.

"Okay, Hawk. Are you ready?" Ava asks, appearing at the entrance to my booth.

"All right, set your notebook down there and hop up here on my chair," I say, slipping on my gloves.

"What?" she asks.

"You want to see what I do, right?" I say.

Ava climbs up on the chair, full of trust and curiosity.

"Now, normally I'd tattoo a person with ink and some needles and this gun," I say, holding up my machine. When her eyes grow wide and she shrinks into the chair, I add, "But not this time."

I turn and push my small cart up next to the chair, showing her an assortment of temporary tattoos sitting next to a dish of warm soapy water and some paper towels.

Ava's eyes grow wide again, but with excitement instead of panic. I press my finger over my lips, the universal sign to *shh* so Drew doesn't hear us, and Ava stifles her giggles.

Then, I get to work on the master plan I hatched yesterday. Meanwhile, Ava asks me her questions more as a cover-up than anything else.

A short while later, we're finished. I wipe her arm and throw all the scraps of paper in the trash. Then we stand and walk out of my booth.

"Mom, I'm all done here," Ava says, clearly trying to keep her voice steady.

Drew turns toward us and does a double take. Ava's once-bare arm is now covered in temporary tattoos, from shoulder to wrist. I gave the kid my first ever temporary full sleeve.

"Oh my god," Drew says.

Shit. What if she's pissed? It dawns on me that I didn't think this through. Maybe I should have asked permission. Then she starts laughing and I exhale the breath I'd been holding.

"Do you like it?" Ava asks.

"It's awesome, kiddo," Drew says, smiling first at Ava, then at me.

I'm smiling too. And fuck, then we're just standing there smiling at each other. For like, a while.

"I'm hungry," I hear Ava say, cutting through whatever the fuck is happening.

Drew drops her gaze and starts nodding to Ava. "Okay, wanna get some dinner?"

"Yeah, but can Hawk come? Please? Please? Hawk, can you come too?" Ava says.

She puts her little hand in mine and looks up at me with pleading eyes.

I didn't realize it before, but she has the same honey glow in her eyes as her mother does. It throws me slightly off balance, in a completely different way. Because I don't understand how this little girl's father doesn't want to be a part of her life.

Ava is the best. And if I can accomplish anything at all, I want her to know she has a friend in me.

WONDER IF YOU WONDER
DREW

When Ava asked Hawk to come with us to dinner, I fully expected him to politely decline. But he didn't. When he offered to take charge of dinner plans, I also fully expected him to take us for a meal that came in wrappers and paper sacks. But he didn't. Instead, we're sitting in his apartment and Ava's playing with his dogs, while I sit perched on a stool at the bar and this motherfucker is cooking with his hands.

With. His. Hands.

For the record, Curtis didn't know how to cook. I don't know any men that know how to cook. So as I watch Hawk chop and sauté, and drop noodles into boiling water, I'm strangely intrigued and a little—dare I say—aroused.

Initially, after the Nina debacle, I fully intended to only ever return to his apartment to pick up Ava or *maybe* if I had a broken bone.

Now, I glance back to see Ava lounging with Raven and Sadie. The three of them have become fast friends, though I doubt anyone would believe me if I told them Ava made friends with two giant pitbulls. I've never been afraid of them but I know many have their opinions based on a stereotype.

"More wine?" Hawk asks me, interrupting my thoughts.

I peer down at my nearly empty glass and nod, thankful my main mode of transportation is walking and home isn't that far. "Sure," I say.

Hawk tips the bottle and pours white wine into my glass about halfway up before setting the bottle down and turning his attention back to the cutting board.

I'm almost mesmerized watching his hands work, and I've caught myself needing to stop staring a few times.

He takes a drink of a clear liquid, likely vodka, from his own glass and puts it back down, briefly making eye contact as he does. "So, did Will get a chance to show you the space next door that we're expanding into?"

"No, actually. We ran out of time this week and we're going to have to do it next week."

This week had been too busy with appointments and walk-ins, and Will had more vendor meetings than she expected. We simply hadn't gotten around to it.

"I could show you after dinner, if you want?" he offers.

"Sure, if you want to. I've been dying to see it," I say, allowing a little excitement to slip out in my tone.

He nods, his lips still pressed into a line but less severe than normal.

We all eat at the bar, and Ava's legs dangle from her stool. Both dogs sit underneath her, appearing as if they silently hope she'll drop something from her plate. Hawk tells Ava about some of the funniest tattoos he's given people. Well, the ones that are appropriate for her to hear about, anyway. Her favorite is the guy who wanted a giant Mickey Mouse head on his stomach with his chest muscles being the ears. He wanted to flex his pecs in and out and make Mickey's ear wiggle. She laughed so hard she nearly choked on her garlic bread.

Did I mention the garlic bread was homemade? With some kind of homemade spread? No, no, not out of a box from the freezer section.

I watch the animation in his face while he tells her, the way his features soften each time he's engaging with Ava. His eyes light up, his lips no longer pressed into a line but curled up at the edges. I listen to his laugh, blending with Ava's in the space between us. Melodic. Deep and soft and smooth.

I realize, somewhere between him showing up at my doorstep with her sketchpad and this moment now, Hawk is so much more than his cold exterior—more than his brooding and sulking. His hard-set jaw is nothing more than a defense mechanism. And slowly but surely, the walls seem to be lowering.

I don't know what's on the other side, but there's a part of me—I don't know how large—that wants to find out.

———

AFTER DINNER, I HELP HAWK CLEAR THE PLATES AND even though he insists I don't, I insist harder on helping because it's the least I can do after he cooked for us. Ava sits on the couch while we rinse the dishes and place them into the dishwasher but, by the time we finish, she's fallen fast asleep.

"Oh dear," I say.

"Just leave her there while I show you the space," he offers. "Then I'll help you get her home."

I nod, and we slowly slip out the door, locking it behind us. We're only going right downstairs after all. Plus, I have a pretty good feeling a fly couldn't land on her without Raven and Sadie knowing something about it.

We walk past the back door of the shop and to the next entrance, where Hawk pulls a key from his pocket and unlocks it, signaling for me to step inside. I walk into the empty space, noticing there's a partially deconstructed kitchen area.

"This was a bakery before. The contractors are working on taking out the kitchen first," he says.

I nod and walk through to the front area, where he starts to point and explain.

"All the tattoo artists are also amazing traditional artists, so on this wall, they'll be able to display canvases and sell them if they want," he says, as he points to the wall furthest from us.

"Up front, I want to have more merchandise than we have now. Apparel and totes and stickers. All kinds of stuff," he adds. "Then I want two more artist stations and maybe an additional counter for piercing jewelry and a piercing room in the back."

"Offering piercing would be cool," I say, looking around and picturing it.

I walk all the way to the front of the space and peer out the windows. I can feel Hawk's eyes on the back of me.

I hear Hawk's boots echoing across the hardwood floors, the empty space a perfect sounding board to unnerve me. My arms instinctively cross over my middle as I feel him settle close behind me, likely only inches away.

If I concentrate hard enough, I can feel his breath move my hair on every exhale.

"Do you like it?" he asks.

"I think it's going to be really great," I say.

"Do you like working here?"

"I really do," I say, with the most sincerity I can muster.

Silence surrounds us and several seconds go by, stretching into minutes.

"Do you like me?" he asks.

His question startles me and I turn my head to look at him, unsure of his meaning or how to answer.

His eyes are practically glowing in the dim space, illuminated by the rays of light filtering in from the streetlamps on the sidewalk outside. *That damn electric blue.*

"Of course, I like you, Hawk. You've been really nice to me and Ava," I assure him.

There's something about the way his eyes squint just a fraction, his lips parting like he's going to say something, but then he presses them together. It leads me to believe that wasn't the answer he was looking for.

Hawk looks out the window as I've been, and I watch his jaw work, studying the muscles in his throat for probably a moment too long.

He pulls his hand up and rubs the back of his neck. "I guess we should get back to Ava," he says.

I nod because I literally don't know what else to do.

We walk back to his apartment in silence and the entire time I wonder if maybe he meant something else, something more, when he asked me that last question.

I allow myself to wonder, for a moment, if he meant as more than a friend.

THE ROAD I'M ON
HAWK

The dogs jump up into the back of the Jeep because, yes, I live in the city, but still insist on owning a vehicle. Sometimes I want to leave this concrete box. Like today. I set the cooler on the back floorboard and pull out onto the street to go pick up Drew and Ava.

What possessed me to do this? I don't know. *Why do I think this will be a good idea?* Again, I have no idea. But I think Ava will enjoy it, and dammit, kids deserve joy. Especially her.

I park on the side of the street and pat Sadie and Raven, assuring them I'll be back in just a few minutes, before I climb the stairs to Drew's second floor apartment. I'm not going to lie. I don't like this apartment building. It's a little shady. Granted, it seems like quite a few older people live here. But also, a lot of less-than-savory people live in the area, too. I hope they keep to themselves and remind myself to ask Drew if they've ever given her any trouble.

Three knocks and several seconds later, I'm greeted by Ava, who's wearing shorts and a T-shirt with sneakers as instructed.

"Hey, Hawk!" She grips my hand, pulling me into the apartment. "Come in. Mom's still getting ready."

I take a seat on their ugly green couch like I did the other night and it's just as unpleasant as I remember. It's as itchy and uncomfortable as it is ugly but I control myself.

Ava sits next to me and pulls her sketchbook up in her lap. "Look what I've been working on!" she exclaims, flipping to what I assume is her newest creation.

I have to admit, the kid has talent. A lot more talent than I had at her age.

"I see you're getting the hang of those pencils I gave ya," I say, rubbing the top of her head and ruffling her hair as Ava giggles.

"What are you two carrying on about?" Drew's voice carries in from the hallway and my eyes jerk up to find her standing there, adjusting her wristwatch.

I take in her form all at once. From her Vans sneakers, up her bare legs, to her tank top that exposes her clavicle bones, and part of me just really likes the way they look. I want to touch them, or tattoo them. I can't decide. Probably both, though.

"Hey," I manage, swallowing hard. *Pull yourself to-fucking-gether, man.* Okay, yes, so Drew's attractive. That's fine. *You've seen attractive women before. Store it away and just focus, for fuck's sake.*

"Hey there," she says, smiling at us.

Before I can stop myself, I stand and walk toward her. I lean in and press a kiss against her cheek. I don't know why I do it. I didn't give it any thought. Her hand comes up to where my lips touched her skin and she cradles it, her pale flesh flushing pink with heat. And I really, *really* like that.

"Ready to go?" I ask.

She nods and collects a small tote, letting Ava put her sketchbook and pencil pouch inside before we head down.

"Wow, you drive a monster truck!" Ava says when she sees my Jeep.

I suppose to her, the lifted off-road vehicle would look like a monster truck. Then again, it might be because it's matte black with matte black rims and dark windows. I guess it does look a little menacing.

"Hop in, little lady," I say, opening the door and holding my hand out to her. I help her in and watch as Sadie and Raven wiggle with excitement to see her.

"Make sure you buckle up," Drew reminds Ava.

"And now you," I say to Drew, extending my hand to her to help her into the front seat.

She steps forward and presses her hand into mine. It's soft and small. My large, calloused hand envelops hers completely. She settles into the passenger seat, and when she looks at me and stifles a grin, I realize I still have a hold of her hand.

"Oh, right." I laugh, releasing my grip.

I shut the door and jog around to the driver's side. Once I hop in, I rub my hands together.

"So, where are we headed?" Drew asks.

"Well, I hope you like road trips and tunes, because we have a little drive ahead of us," I say, smiling as I pull out onto the road.

———

AVA'S A BANGER. DREW SEEMS JUST AS SURPRISED BY IT as I am. We both take turns peeking back at her small frame, while she's banging her head up and down to my *awesome rock and roll music* as she called it. In truth, I played Chevelle, Pop Evil, and some other similar stuff.

We head out of the city and a little way's south for a couple of hours, making our way to the conservatory. Things are slower out here, a bit calmer. We finally pull up to our destination and despite the long drive, Ava's been so excited, she didn't complain one time.

After helping Drew and Ava out, I leash the dogs and start walking.

"Where are we?" Drew asks.

"A park," I say, watching as Drew looks around, taking it all in. There are small buildings, picnic areas, fenced in areas, and wooded trails along the edges.

"Don't worry, we're just dropping the dogs off and then we have something to see," I say.

We round the corner and my fur girls immediately start wiggling their butts.

"A dog park!" Ava exclaims.

"The dogs can play here while I show you one of my favorite places," I say, looking down at her.

After signing the dogs in and unleashing them to play, I lead the girls to the building in the center—the one we've come here for.

"What's a con-server-tory?" Ava tries.

"Conservatory," I correct. "A butterfly conservatory, to be exact."

"There's butterflies in there?" Ava asks, her eyes lighting up.

"Yep." I nod. "A whole lot of 'em."

"What are we waiting for?" Ava asks, barely able to contain

THE ROAD I'M ON

her excitement. She grabs one of my hands and one of Drew's, dragging us toward the door.

Our bodies lurch forward to keep up with the super strength of an excited child and once we're inside, we begin to navigate the halls of the conservatory. Butterflies circle above us freely, filling the space with bright colors, all swirling together.

We walk through as Ava stops at each glass display with reptiles and snakes. She takes a particular liking to the pale-yellow corn snakes. The blue geckos seem to be Drew's favorite as they slither over rocks and bop their snouts against the glass where her hand is. My personal favorite are the small brown bats in the dark room toward the end. They hang upside down under a black light. They're practically tiny puppies with wings.

Ava looks on with fascination, never letting go of my hand, or Drew's for that matter. We're a human chain. Ava's the little middle link, binding us all together, steering us from one exhibit to the next.

From time to time, Drew's eyes meet mine and she smiles. Then I realize it's me that's smiling. For a split second, I think we're having some kind of moment. Until Ava drags us away to the next thing.

Of course we're not having a moment. That would be ridiculous. I don't think Drew sees me like that. As a matter of fact, until recently, she probably thought I was kind of a dick. I hope she sees me as a nice guy now, or at least a nice boss.

The next thing I know, we're exiting the building, still linked together, and I realize to anyone passing us what we must look like. To any stranger who doesn't know who we are, what we actually are. Hand in hand like this, it hits me that we look like a family.

WAKING LIONS
DREW

We sit down at a picnic table and Hawk produces a cooler I hadn't even realized was in his Jeep. He really did have this whole thing planned. From where we're sitting, we can see into the fenced area where all the dogs are playing. Sadie and Raven are having a blast, and something tells me they'll be sleeping hard on the trip back home. For that matter, it's possible Ava will be too.

"This is for you," he says, placing a Tupperware container in front of me. "And this is for you," he says to Ava, placing one in front of her. Hawk pulls out his own container last, then places drinks in front of us.

"Wow, I get a Coke? Best day ever!" Ava says.

"Crap, I guess I should've asked," Hawk says, shooting me a look.

"It's fine," I say, reaching for his forearm and squeezing, attempting to reassure him.

We open our containers, and while he and I have a more adult selection—which includes the most delicious looking chicken salad sandwiches on croissants and sides of pasta salad—I see he's taken care to pack Ava a peanut butter and jelly with grapes and string cheese.

"Is that okay?" he asks her.

Ava nods vigorously and bites into her sandwich, her eyes growing wide. "Mom! This is crunchy peanut butter and strawberry jam!"

I laugh and look at Hawk, who looks pleased with himself. I'm pleased with him, too. *Full of surprises, this one.*

We settle into easy conversation as we eat our lunch. Ava takes center stage for most of the conversation and entertains us with stories of her school friends and class drama. Well, as much drama as you can have in elementary school. When she's finished, she asks if she can play nearby and I let her, thinking it will be nice to have a moment alone with Hawk.

As I watch her smell the wildflowers blooming, I notice Hawk is watching her too.

"Thank you for today," I say. I take notice I'm thanking him a lot lately.

"Of course," he says. "I'm having a lot of fun."

"Can I ask you a question?" I'm hesitant to ask anything too personal but the itch has been there too long.

"Of course," he repeats.

"Why did it make you so mad? Hearing about Ava's father?"

Hawk stiffens a bit, biting his bottom lip like he's wondering if he should answer. "My mother was a single mom, too. She raised me and my older brother by herself," he says.

"Oh," I say. "And you just—"

"And, I just get it. And it makes me as angry as my own father did," he says.

"Do you talk to your father at all?"

"I can count on both hands how many times I saw him up until I turned eighteen. Then I stopped talking to him. Then, he died," he says, no emotion in his voice.

I gasp. "Oh my god, I'm so sorry."

"Don't be. He wasn't a dad to me or my brother. He gave my mom some money sometimes. And when he died, my brother and I got insurance money. That's it." Hawk's shoulders bunch up and then fall.

It's less of a shrug and more a show of defeat. I know he says he doesn't care, but it feels like he does.

"You can still be sad about it. You can still feel sad."

"I'd rather not," he says. "What about you?"

"Me?"

"Your parents," he clarifies.

"My parents died when I was like, two. I don't remember them at all. I think I stayed here with my Aunt Penny for a while until she couldn't do it anymore. So I was put in foster care."

Shock is splashed all over Hawk's face, his eyes silently urging me to go on.

"I got adopted eventually. They were nice enough but we never quite bonded, if that makes sense. So I went to college, and I think that's why when I met Curtis and got pregnant I just clung to the idea of a family so hard. I'd never really had much of one, so I wanted to make my own."

Hawk nods. "I understand."

"Yeah?"

"Yeah, and so will anyone at Bird's Eye. Because that's what we did. We made our own family," he says.

I let his words sink in, recalling vague details of passing

conversations I've had with each person there, and he's right. Will's stressed relationship with her parents. Avery's abusive father. Hanson's mother was an addict, I think. All of them, cast out or down by their families in some way. Now, they're together, made whole by choice.

Ava runs over, interrupting our intense moment, huffing out exasperated breaths. It seems like she's been running a marathon.

"Can I draw now?" she asks, sitting back down at the picnic table and taking a big gulp of her Coke.

I reach into the tote I brought and pull out her book and pencils. She flips open to a new page, but not before the drawing on the page just before it catches my eye.

"What's that?" I ask.

"That's nothing," she says.

Ava's never been one to hide her sketches. She's always so proud of them and wants to show them off.

"Come on, show us," I say.

I watch her gulp and shift her stare from me to Hawk. Hawk looks from Ava to me, his curiosity just as palpable as mine. Ava reluctantly flips the page back, revealing a drawing of Hawk. It's definitely Hawk because his tattoos are all over. And it's good— really good. She captured his sharp jaw, his slicked hair, his wide shoulders.

"I thought it would be fun to try to draw your tattoos. I'm sorry," she says, her eyes downcast.

"Ava, why are you sorry?" he asks, tilting his head toward her.

"I don't want you to be mad at me," she says.

"I could never be mad at you for this, Ava," he says, pulling her chin up so she looks at him. "This is amazing. No one has ever drawn me before."

"Really?" Her eyes start to sparkle again as the sadness quickly melts away from her face.

My insides are a puddle, but I hold it together as I watch this scene unfold.

"I promise, kid," he assures her.

I can't say for certain when things began to shift. Maybe it was before now, maybe it was quietly happening in the background the entire time. But as I watch Hawk lean over Ava's sketch with her, pointing and laughing and drawing, I'm overcome with emotion. Happiness. Fear. Excitement. Anxiety.

Wow, that's a lot of emotions.

Though, somewhere deep down inside me, I hear the crackling of embers. The remnants of a fire that once burned so bright inside me, stomped out long ago. I didn't think anything was left. But here he is, unknowingly digging through rubble, fanning an all but dead flame.

NO REGRETS
HAWK

Do it. Just do it, man. Focus. Say it.

"I hope Ava had a good time today," I say instead, standing at Drew's door.

After helping her get a sleeping Ava into the apartment, along with her tote, I've been standing here making small talk for longer than necessary. I honestly don't know what's happening to me right now. I can't even ask a simple fucking question.

"Yeah, she had a blast," Drew says. "Thank you again."

She looks up at me, her eyes dancing and, if I'm reading the situation right, almost expectant. She's leaning toward me and I could do it. I could reach out and touch her face, run my thumb over her jawline, brush my lips against hers. *Okay, no.*

"Do you want to go somewhere with me tomorrow night?" I ask, biting my bottom lip.

"Just me?"

"I have a babysitter, if that's what you're worried about," I reassure her, and her eyes narrow. "Someone you know."

"All right," she says.

"Yes?" I confirm.

"Yes. Where are we going?" she asks, giggling.

"I can't tell you that."

"Well, what should I wear?"

I rub my chin, peering up, really putting on a show. "Something…spicy."

"Spicy?" she repeats.

I watch her gulp, watch the slightest hint of color fill her cheeks, and I wink at her. "Yes, Drew. Spicy." I smile.

She silently nods to me, absorbing my words. Or rather, the single word I've used to render her speechless.

I tell her I'll pick her up at seven and head down to my Jeep, retrieving my phone from my front pocket while I hop in.

Me: I need a favor.

Will: Did you kiss her yet?

Me: I'm working on it.

———

WHY I'M NERVOUS IS A RIDDLE TO ME. A FUCKING riddle, I tell you. I'm not a nervous guy. Women don't unnerve me. Going on dates is generally a breeze for me. But, Drew is different. She *feels* different. I steady my hands as I stand outside her door before I knock, a bouquet of orchids in my grip.

I finally knock and wait a beat before Ava answers the door.

"Hawk!" she says.

"Hey, kid," I say, giving her a smile and ruffling her hair.

She grabs my hand and leads me into the living room. I take my familiar seat on the couch as she explains that Will and Drew are in the bedroom.

"Will has been here *forrreverrr* helping Mom get ready," she says. *Leave it to the kid for honesty.* "Are those for mom?" She points at the orchids, her eyes lighting up.

"You think she'll like them?" I ask.

Ava nods her head, and we both turn as we hear the faint click of the bedroom door. I stand, swallowing hard.

Will walks out first, looking pleased with herself. I give a nod to my old friend. She always comes through for me. But my eyes are fixed beyond her, over her shoulder.

The blonde cascade of waves flowing across bare clavicle bones catches my attention first. The deep red off the shoulder straps wraps around Drew's upper arms. Soft looking fabric hugs all the way from her breasts down to just above her knees, every curve on display. She's wearing black platform heels, bringing her much closer to my height, and I forget we're not alone for a moment too long.

I step closer to her, looking at her face. Her makeup is subtle, with the exception of the painted lips. A dark red shade, perfectly matching her dress. *Oh, the lips.* I take in all of Drew, savoring the moment. Because she is a fucking vision. The animal inside me wants to smudge her red lips, wants to grab her by the throat and rub my thumb across them until it's nearly gone. *And holy shit, snap out of it.*

"Hello," I say, handing her the orchids.

"Hey there," she says, her eyes falling over my body in what feels like the same sort of assessment I'd just given her.

"Okay, you two. Have fun, stay out late. You know what, stay out all night. We'll be fine here. Right, Ava?" Will says, ushering us toward the door and taking the flowers from Drew's hand.

"Right!" Ava says, waving at us from the couch.

The next thing I know, we're in the hallway and alone and I'm thinking about all the ways I want to kiss her, but I don't. I lead her to my Jeep, help her in, and get behind the wheel.

"Do you like jazz music and Italian food?" I ask.

"Love both," she says.

"Great, but we can't drink," I tell her firmly.

"Oh, okay," she says, confusion playing in her voice.

"You trust me, don't you?" I ask.

"Yes," she says.

"Good," I say. And then, I test the water. I reach across the middle console and slip my hand into hers, intertwining our fingers.

She doesn't pull back or hesitate. She gives her palm to me, laces her fingers between mine, and I watch from the corner of my eye as a smile spreads across her painted mouth.

CAN WE KISS FOREVER?

DREW

Let's recap, shall we?

As soon as Hawk asked me to wear something spicy and left, I immediately texted Will because what the fuck does *spicy* mean? I've been a mother since I was nineteen. Am I supposed to fucking put hot sauce in my pocket?

She took me to what she called *the fancy thrift store in the rich neighborhood* and I walked away with a stunning red dress and black heels. I'm not even going to comment about how I feel in them just yet.

Then we spent what felt like a millennium painting my face and curling my hair just right. All the while, she's reassuring me that *this* is *spicy*.

But then I walk out into my living room. And Hawk's jaw is nearly unhinged. And he's looking at me like he's never looked at me before. Like he's hungry. Like he wants to touch me. And I'm looking at him because he's wearing tight black jeans and black boots and the whitest pressed V-neck T-shirt I've ever seen. And over it? A leather jacket. *A fucking leather jacket.*

His hair is slick and his tattoos are peeking out of the top of his shirt and crawling up his throat and every time he swallows, I think an angel gets its wings or something. But right, he's staring at me with those electric blue eyes and I can feel my heart in my throat and things fluttering everywhere.

Before I know it, we're out the door.

We're holding hands in his car. *Holding hands!*

At the restaurant, perfect smooth jazz plays, and low lighting cradles us. A single candle on our table illuminates Hawk's face so subtly and, I swear I've never seen him more relaxed. Our food is perfect and as he requested, we both drink water.

Which brings us to now.

I'm sitting in Hawk's tattoo chair, the glow of his lamp the only light on in Bird's Eye Tattoo Studio. I watch him pour ink into little cups and place needles into his gun. He pulls black gloves on and rubs balm over my collarbone.

He lays a stencil of the constellation Orion over my skin, the bottom of it hitting the top of my breast and wrapping up to the top of my shoulder. Orion's Belt sits across my clavicle and the hunter's bow is pointed inward, toward my chest. It's only small stars and delicate lines, but I'm nervous.

Maybe it's a little about getting tattooed. But I think it's more about who's doing it. And his proximity.

"You ready?" Hawk asks.

"As ready as I'll ever be," I say, gripping the chair's arms and laying my head back.

"Just breathe," he says, so that's exactly what I do.

Then, he leans in close, and breathing becomes a little diffi-cult. Hawk's face is inches from mine as he hovers over my shoulder and presses the tip of his gun to my skin. The wave of vibrating pain numbs me almost immediately.

"Is that okay?" he asks, not taking his eyes away from his work.

"Yes," I whisper, trying to keep my breath steady and movement minimal.

"It's not good to drink before you get a tattoo. It can cause you to bleed more," he says, as he wipes at my skin and dips his needle again.

"Thank you for being so professional," I say.

"I may be many unsavory things, but I take tattooing seriously," he says.

"I don't think you're unsavory," I say. I hear the gun stop moving as his eyes meet mine.

"You don't?" he asks.

I shake my head, unable to break eye contact. My lips part slightly and I can barely contain myself. My heart is beating so hard he might even be able to see it pounding in my chest. My skin is hot, and I pray it isn't turning red.

The gun starts again and he looks back down, tracing more lines in silence. I lean back and close my eyes. Time passes without indication until he announces he's finished.

"You didn't really bleed much at all and this shouldn't leak too bad since it's delicate, but I'm going to put a bandage over it so the balm doesn't get on your dress," he says.

He uses two fingers to gently coat the affected skin in the aforementioned balm, then places a bandage over the area and tapes around the edges after showing me the finished piece in a mirror.

"What do you think?" he asks.

"I love it," I say. "Thank you so much."

Hawk stands and pulls his gloves from his hands, tossing them into the trash can.

"It's no problem. Happy to defile your skin, anytime," he says.

Defile. Oh my.

"Oh, and we can get a drink now, if you want." His eyes search mine, his lips parted and pulled up into a grin.

"All right." I rub my arms, suddenly shivering. *Am I cold? Is something wrong with the temperature in here? What's going on?*

"Here," he says, pulling his jacket from the back of his chair and draping it over my shoulders.

I can smell him on the worn black leather. Spice and clean soap. I try to disguise the fact that I'm inhaling deeply, over and over.

He takes my hand in his again, leading me out the back door and up the stairs to his apartment. And suddenly, I find it hard to breathe again. Maybe it's this dress. Maybe it's the city smog. Air pollution is a real thing. Maybe it's the *what if*, the possibility of what might happen.

Hawk unlocks the door, leading me inside. I hear the click of the door shutting behind me and it sounds so loud against the silence of his apartment.

"I'll put some music on," he says. He grabs a remote from the counter and clicks a couple of buttons until the space fills with smooth, sexy music.

He walks into the kitchen and pours me a glass of wine, and himself a vodka. He steps closer to hand me the glass, then holds his vodka out toward me. "Cheers," he says.

"To what?" I ask.

"The string of events that led us here," he says. And despite the rough journey, I have to agree. I clink my glass gently against his and take a sip.

A new song begins to play, one I've never heard, and I really like it. "What is this?" I ask.

Hawk's ears perk up and he smiles. "*Pills,* by Denim Blue and Miclain Keith." He takes another gulp of his vodka then reaches for my glass, setting both down on the counter. "Dance with me," he says, stepping toward me with his arms out.

I put my hands up as he reaches for them, wrapping them around his neck. His hands glide down over my ribs and settle on my hips, as he guides me from side to side. I swear I've only had a few sips of wine, but I feel very hot and very drunk. He leans down, resting his cheek against mine, and his hot breath hits my ear.

"What are you thinking?" I ask, swallowing to try to remedy the sudden dry mouth I have.

Hawk is silent for several moments, only this song and his inhale and exhale filling the air. "I'm thinking this feels really good. I'm thinking of a hundred different ways I'd like to kiss you. And I'm thinking I don't want to mess this up," he admits.

I exhale sharply, realizing I'd been holding my breath while listening to him speak. His hands slide from my hip to the small of my back and pull me in closer, against his chest.

"Drew?" he whispers.

"Yes?" I whisper back against his jaw.

"Let me kiss you." His words fall out more as a statement than a request.

Hawk's other hand slides up the length of my body, cradling my jaw in such a way, I feel his fingertips pressed into the nape of my neck, his thumb over my chin. He pulls back, his eyes locked with mine, waiting for permission.

"Yes," I whisper, my voice barely audible.

His thumb presses against the center of my closed lips, then drags across my skin, smudging the slick red.

"I've wanted to do that all night," he whispers, as his lips move closer to mine.

His hand moves lower against my throat, applying the lightest amount of pressure as he finally presses his lips against mine. They're full and soft as he exhales against my mouth.

A moan escapes me and *dear god*, I think it awakens something in him. His grip around my throat tightens a little more, his tongue parting my lips. Not that I'm complaining, because *holy shit*.

My hands grab fistfuls of the back of his shirt and hang on for dear life, because I hope this ride is far from over.

WHEN THE LIGHTS GO DOWN
HAWK

Before I can stop myself, I back Drew up against the nearest wall, pressing into her because she feels so fucking *good*. I tilt her head back further, biting and sucking on her lips until I finally manage to break the kiss, moving my mouth to her exposed throat. I lick and suck, bite and kiss, living for the noises coming from inside of her.

She is divine. Watching her flesh turn pink drives me wild.

Drew claws at my back and I don't know if she's spurring me on intentionally but I am an animal unleashed. I kiss lower, bite her clavicle, licking the top of her tits.

Oh my god, what the hell am I doing? Using the wall behind her, I push away, taking several deep breaths. The sound of her panting is all I can hear but my eyes are fixed on the floor, because if I look at her, I will attack again.

"What's wrong?" she asks.

Oh Jesus. "God, nothing. Everything. I want you," I confess.

I'm wondering if that sounded more pathetic out loud than in my head. I'm wondering if I've gone too far.

"Take me," she says, so maybe I didn't press my luck after all.

I waste no time, rushing back, pressing into her, taking her by the mouth again. I bend down just enough to run my fingers underneath the edge of her dress, hiking it up so I can wrap her thighs around my waist. Lifting her with ease, I cup her ass as she moans into my mouth again and I swear to god, I might lose it right here against the wall in my living room.

Her thighs tighten around me, her hands running through my hair as I carry her down the hall. I push my bedroom door open and walk to the edge of my bed, laying her down and standing over her. She's looking up at me, hunger in her eyes. I'm desperate for this moment, consumed by want.

"Are you sure?" I ask.

She nods her head softly and I pull my shirt off. I watch her eyes move over my skin, bounce from one tattoo to the next, tracing over each one. I lift one of her feet up and then the other, removing her high heels, kissing her ankles before I place them back on the bed.

"Drew?"

"Yes?" she whispers, as I lower down closer to her.

"I really want to see your other tattoo," I say, tucking her hair behind her ear and grinning.

"Go find it," she whispers.

A chill runs down my spine. *She. Is. A. Devil. Woman.*

I kneel at the foot of my bed, softly kissing the insides of her knees, spreading her legs a little wider. I push the dress higher, kissing a trail over her thighs until I find the little bird. A small sparrow sits right where her thigh meets her hip. She giggles as I press my lips to it.

Then I place a kiss on top of her panties, but she doesn't

laugh this time. She grips the bed sheets as her breathing gets faster and harder. I can feel her body resisting the urge to arch toward me, to invite more touch.

I prop myself up enough to look into her hooded honey eyes, darkened and swirling. My thumbs hook into the edge of her lace panties, and I slide them down until they fall to the floor. My hands cup her ass as I gaze down at her sensitive flash. I'm fucking salivating.

"Hawk?" Drew's voice cuts through my focus and I look up at her. "Just because I don't have a bunch of tattoos doesn't mean you have to be gentle," she says, no hesitation in her tone.

Oh, fuck. Challenge accepted.

I lower and lick the center of her slowly, then blow. She arches and moans. I lick again, swirling my tongue in circles until I feel her legs start to shake. Then I pull away and blow against her skin again. She moans louder, covering her mouth.

"No one can hear you," I whisper against her.

She moves her hand back to the sheets, gripping them tighter.

I lick again then suck on her clit, lapping my tongue against her over and over, her back arching, legs wobbling. Drew presses herself into my mouth, a plea for more.

"Hawk, please," she begs.

"What?" I ask, blowing against her again.

"I want you," she says, reaching down for me.

"What do you want, babe? I ask.

"I want you inside me. I want all of you," she says.

Licking the taste of her from my lips, I stand and start to unbuckle my pants. She sits up and unzips the side of her dress, pulling the sleeves down, exposing her tits. *Perfection.*

Drew throws her dress to the floor as the streetlights filter in from the window, illuminating her porcelain flesh and I'm mesmerized by her. *Milky skin. Honey eyes. So sweet.*

Drew scoots to the edge of the bed and picks up where I'm frozen in place, continuing to unbuckle my pants. I drop my hands to my sides, letting her take the lead. She unzips me, hooking her hands into the top of my briefs and pants at the same time, pulling everything down in one fluid motion.

All at once, I'm exposed and she wraps her hand around me, looking up at me. I didn't know it was possible for someone to look so angelic and so devilish at the same time.

She takes my dick into her mouth and it takes all my concentration not to come the instant I feel her tongue against me. Because to hell with ninety-nine virgins. If there's a heaven and I get to go, I want this. Exactly this.

After a few minutes, she stops and lies back on the bed, shifting until she hits the pillows. She puts her hands behind her head and stares at me.

"Well. I'm waiting." She giggles.

I grab a condom from the dresser, ripping it open and sliding it on. I turn and crawl up the bed toward her, lowering and wrapping my arms around her. I kiss her breasts, suck on her nipples, trail my tongue up her sternum. She moans again and I growl. It's guttural, from somewhere inside my chest.

Her legs part and hook around me as I lower myself closer. I rub against her, savoring the tease, the way her body arches, one more time. Then I push into her slowly, completely, listening to her sharp inhale against my chest. I slide out and back in again, disappearing into her.

Our hips grind together until we find a comfortable rhythm. Her moans grow stronger and deeper until she's nearly screaming. I press into her, harder and faster, reaching for her tits. I smash my mouth against hers, parting her lips with my tongue again, kissing her moans away.

"I'm gonna come," she says against my mouth as I lose myself deeper inside her.

"Yes, come for me," I beg.

I feel her body shudder against mine, clenching and twisting with pleasure. She stiffens, then relaxes, and only then do I succumb to my own desires. Holding her tight, I come for her, because of her. Then, I collapse, trying to still my ragged breaths.

Drew wraps her arms around me, placing soft kisses against my temple, cheek, and jaw.

Eventually and reluctantly, I roll off her, her body immediately cuddling to my side. We're silent for a long time, both of us just trying to catch our breath. I listen to the rhythmic in and out as they sync up with one another.

"Have you ever noticed how people are like conch shells?" she says.

"Say what?" I ask.

"If you put your ear to their chest like this, you can hear their heart beating and blood swirling and lungs filling up, all at once. There's a whole world inside there," she says, her ear now pressed firmly against my chest.

"I guess I never thought about it," I say. I twirl strands of her hair around my finger and close my eyes, basking in the moment.

"Here, you try it," she says. She lies on her back, inviting me to put my head on her chest, arms open to me.

I twist and roll onto my side, wrapping my arms around her and laying my head on her chest, taking up most of it. "Mmmm, built in pillows," I muse.

She giggles then says, "Listen."

I close my eyes and concentrate on the sounds coming from her chest. I hear her heart beating first, then her lungs filling as she inhales and exhales. A great swirling sound accompanies all of it, much like the sound of the ocean you hear in a conch shell. It really is like there's a whole world inside her chest.

Then it hits me. Drew is a conch shell. Small and delicate, unassuming on the outside. But if you listen closely, a whole world is crashing around on the inside.

PILLOWTALK
HAWK

My face is still nestled between Drew's soft, exquisite breasts as my eyes flutter open. Her heartbeat is considerably slower, breaths steady. *When did we fall asleep?* Hazy daylight filters in from the windows.

"Good morning," she says softly, stretching her arms up over her head.

I prop myself up on my elbow, gazing down at her in the light of the early morning because I believe this is when women are their most vulnerable—and by extension—their most beautiful. The once perfect waves in her hair are now a frizzy mess. The delicate skin around her mouth is swollen from my kisses, stained red from her lipstick. Mascara is smudged under her eyes. She looks up at me, that honey glow never more electric than in this moment. She is a goddess.

"Good morning, beautiful," I say, reaching up and pressing a kiss to her forehead.

"What time is it?" she asks.

I look over her shoulder to the clock on my nightstand. "A little past seven."

"Can you text Will?" she asks. "Just to make sure everything is okay?"

I nod, reaching down to the floor and feeling around the pockets of my pants, finding my phone.

Me: Everything okay over there?

Will: We want to come over for breakfast.

I roll my eyes. Because what she really means is she suggested it to Ava so she could come over and quietly interrogate us and make it awkward for us in front of Ava as a means of torture.

Me: What? No.

Will: It's too late. Ava picked out clothes for Drew and we are grabbing some food and coffee on the way. Be there soon.

I shoot a look back to Drew. "So...up for some company?" I ask her, a nervousness growing in me.

"What do you mean?" she asks.

"Will sort of invited herself and Ava over for breakfast. They're bringing you some clothes, along with breakfast and coffee," I say, wincing. I wait for a reaction, expecting her to panic at least a little.

"Do you have something I can wear until they get here with my clothes?" she asks.

Okay, not what I expected. "You're not upset?" I ask.

"Why would I be upset? All my favorite people will be here for breakfast," she says, leaning up to kiss me on the cheek.

"I didn't know if you'd want to have Ava see us, like...I don't know, you know?" My words trail off because I don't know what the fuck I'm trying to say because I've never done any of this with someone who's had a kid and I don't know what the rules are.

"Well, I mean, I don't want her to see us lying naked in bed, no." She laughs.

I give her that look. You know that *I'm trying to be serious here* look.

"Hawk, listen. She likes you. You guys are buddies. I think it's okay for her to see us hug, hold hands. I mean, maybe we shouldn't kiss in front of her or anything like that? Not yet anyway."

And what she says makes sense. I totally thought I would need to pretend there was an invisible six-inch barrier between us at all times so I'm a little relieved. "Okay, yeah. That's okay with me," I say, after her words still my panic.

"Good. So can I have some clothes now?" she asks.

My eyes slide down over her naked body one last time, committing it to memory. I press my lips into a hard line, exhaling deeply.

"I suppose I can't just keep you locked in my bedroom naked and ready for sex all day," I say, standing from my bed and walking to the dresser.

I hear her push away the sheets and stand then feel her arms wrap around me from the back. She reaches up and grips my chest.

"I promise if I can have clothes now, I'll make up for it later," she whispers, her hot breath hitting my spine.

I turn to face her, looking deep into her eyes. With her heels now gone, I tower over her. "How is this exactly?" I ask.

"You're a psycho, you know that?" She giggles.

"I've been called worse," I say, leaning down, pressing my forehead to hers.

"If I can have clothes now," she says, "I'll let you wear me like a straitjacket later."

Fucking. Deal.

WHERE DID YOU SLEEP LAST NIGHT?
DREW

To literally no one's surprise, Hawk doesn't exactly have clothes that fit me. When Will arrived with Ava, I was wearing one of his T-shirts which swallowed me and a pair of his basketball shorts cinched all the way in and rolled up. So, I guess you could say I was grateful they had enough forethought to bring me clothes.

I exit the bathroom wearing my own leggings and sports bra, but couldn't part with his shirt that smelled like him so I tied a knot at the bottom in the back and decided to go for the Sunday lazy chic look. *Sure, that works.*

"Are you still wearing my shirt?" Hawk asks from the kitchen counter. All eyes are on me as I walk toward them.

"Yep. It's more comfortable," I say, shrugging. He raises an eyebrow at me and I sit on a stool, ignoring his silent accusations. Instead, I grab an iced coffee from the holder and say, "Will, you're a lifesaver for this. In more ways than one." I give her a silent woman-to-woman *thank you.*

"Don't mention it. But tell me, how was your evening?" she

asks, looking between us, resting her elbow on the counter and propping her chin in her hand. Her grin grows wide across her face and I know my chest is getting splotchy; I feel the heat radiating off my skin.

"Yeah, Drew, how was our evening?" Hawk asks.

What the fuck? Okay, I can play too. "Perfectly adequate, thank you."

"Just adequate?" Will asks, shooting Hawk a look of amusement, to which his eyes narrow.

"What did you guys do?" Ava cuts in.

Ugh, this can't be happening. "We had dinner and listened to music," I say, giving her the extremely G-rated censored version.

"Sounds boring." Ava shrugs, causing Will to snicker.

"Well, it's not when you're a grownup," I say.

She shrugs her shoulders again, turning back to her breakfast sandwich and chocolate milk.

"Well, if you ask me," Hawk says, "I think it was a little more than adequate."

"Men always think that," Will says, tilting her head at him.

Hawk looks at me, waiting, like I'm supposed to set the record straight now. Will turns to me. *Oh my god.* My whole face is burning. I can feel it. It's gonna melt off at any moment.

"Hawkward," Will says, shaking her head.

"Did you just smash my name together with the word awkward?" Hawk asks Will.

"Yeah," Will says. "Want me to hashtag it?"

"I wish you wouldn't," he says.

"Hashtag Hawkward." Will laughs. "I like it."

This is getting out of hand. All the while, Ava's just taking bites of her food, completely unaware. The two adults in the room look at me again.

I start to stammer out, "I, uh, I mean…everything was…"

"See," Hawk says.

"Okay, okay," Will says, holding up her hands in defeat. Will comes and stands next to me, wrapping her arm around my shoulder. "You've been rendered speechless, babe. It's okay. We've all been there."

My eyes grow big and I look at Hawk.

"Ew, gross. Not with Hawk. Yuck," she says.

"Hey," Hawk says. "Sheesh."

"I just mean in general," she says.

"Hey, Hawk?" Ava cuts in again, mumbling through a bite of her sandwich.

"What's up, kid?" he replies, before biting into his own sandwich.

"Are you my mom's boyfriend now?" she asks, no pause or hesitation in her voice. Leave it to kids to ask the hard-hitting questions.

If you've never seen a well-muscled, tattooed beast of a man with a hard-set jaw and cold demeanor choke on his food at a simple question by an eight-year-old girl, you should. I highly recommend it. Bits of food fly from his mouth as he gasps and hits his chest. Will and I look on as Ava sips her chocolate milk as if nothing has happened.

Hawk takes a few sips of water and then shoots me a look of *"HELP! WHAT DO I SAY?"* but I just shrug in response, because I don't know what the hell to say either. Plus, I sort of want to watch him squirm.

"Um, well, is that something you would like, or?" he asks Ava.

"I think you would make a good boyfriend and girlfriend," she answers.

Hawk's eyes grow wide and I cover my mouth, looking over at Will who seems pleased as punch as this whole scene unfolds.

"You do? How come?" he asks her.

"Well, you think she's pretty don't you?" she asks.

I swear to god the man turns pink.

"Yes," he says. "Your mom is very pretty."

"And she's nice, and funny. And you're nice and funny. And I know she thinks you're handsome,' she says.

"She does, huh?" he asks her, turning to me and raising an eyebrow.

"Yeah, I heard her tell Will that she thinks you're *yummmm-myyyyyyy*," Ava says.

And then I die. Right there, right then. And my ghost floats up to the ceiling.

"Well, that's good." He laughs, crossing his arms over his chest, looking quite smug.

"And you like me, don't you?" Ava asks him, and my heart actually hurts at her question.

I watch Hawk swallow hard and uncross his arms, walking toward her. He ruffles the top of her head. "Of course, kid," he says. "You're the best."

Ava's eyes light up, and I'm overcome with happiness and fear all at once. Because I've seen that look before. When her father would surprise her with special father-daughter days. When he'd let her stay up and watch a movie with him. When he'd tell her she was his little princess.

That is, until those moments became less and less frequent. After the separation, they stopped altogether. And if her father could rip that away from her, how can I trust another man not to?

"So...?" Ava says.

He gives Ava a long look, studying her face and absorbing her words. "You're right, kid. There's only one logical thing to do." He walks toward me, a smirk playing across his lips.

Oh god. Oh god. Oh god. What's he doing?

He stands in front of me and reaches for my hand. "Drew," he says softly, "will you be my girlfriend?"

I gulp, glancing at Will, whose eyes are as big as mine feel. I look at Ava, who's practically falling out of her seat with anticipation.

"Yes," I say softly.

"Yay!" Ava exclaims. "Now kiss her!"

Oh dear.

TEAR IN MY HEART
DREW

Last week, I was just Drew. This week, I'm still Drew, but I'm also the girlfriend of the very sexy, very smoldering owner of Bird's Eye Tattoo Studio. And it's been a really, really great week for Drew. Work has been steady, and I'm getting used to the rhythm of the shop.

Despite constant begging from both Ava and Hawk, I've resisted their pleas and Ava's requests for all of us to have *slumber parties* at Hawk's apartment every single night.

Except, now it's Friday night. And my *not on a school night* excuse is out the window. So here she stands at the front counter of Bird's Eye, waiting for my answer. Because the *no minors in the shop* rule doesn't apply to the daughter of the girlfriend of King Hawk. And right next to her, Hawk is standing with his hand on her shoulder in full support of her mission.

"I bought movie snacks," he says.

"Please, please, please Mom?" Ava says, her hands clasped together so tightly her knuckles are starting to turn white.

"And we can rent the new *Frozen* movie," he says.

Ava's eyes grow as big as saucers and I know I've officially lost.

"Okay, we can have a slumber party," I relent.

"Yes!" she yells.

"Oh, and would you look here?" I say, pulling out the overnight bag I've had stashed behind the front counter all day. "I've come prepared."

Hawk smiles at me, his pearly whites sinking into his bottom lip.

We close up the shop and head upstairs to his apartment early, where we're greeted at the door by Raven and Sadie, wiggling their entire bodies and licking Ava like it's been a month since they've seen her.

"Hey, Ava? You wanna build a fort in the living room?" Hawk asks.

If my kid's jaw dropped any lower, I'd be scraping it off the floor with a spatula.

"The hall closet should have everything we need," he says, pointing down the hall.

Ava runs like she's on fire, returning with her arms loaded with as many blankets and sheets as her little body can carry. Then she runs back for more.

Hawk rips the cushions from the couch and gathers all the pillows in the entire apartment, but they both insist they've got a handle on this and I should be in charge of the snacks. So I get to work preparing bowls of popcorn, bags of candy, and a plate of miniature sandwiches. I even use a giant bowl for a makeshift cooler for the sodas and juice boxes.

"All done," Ava exclaims.

I turn and peer into the living room at the biggest blanket fort

I've ever seen. It stretches from the back of the couch over the entire living room area to the wall the television is on, so that the TV is actually inside the fort. "Whoa," is all I can manage.

"Pretty awesome, huh?" Hawk says.

"That's seriously impressive," I say.

"It's not my first time," he says, and now I'm thinking about what other time Hawk would have been making blanket forts.

We take turns changing into our pajamas and then it's time for the main event.

We all climb in and, as promised, Hawk rents *Frozen II*. Even Raven and Sadie curl up inside. Ava is lying between me and Hawk, watching the movie with intense concentration for about five seconds until Hawk interjects.

While I glance at the movie from time to time, I find myself watching Hawk and Ava more. They laugh and high five, he tickles her, she punches him in the arm. He bops her on the nose and she tries throwing popcorn into his mouth. She finally turns her eyes back to the movie and his catch mine, a smile blooming on his lips. He mouths me a silent *hi* and I do the same back. He reaches for me, tucking my hair behind my ear then bops my nose too. I scrunch it and smile.

We all fall into silence, listening to Anna and Elsa save their world yet again. Before too long, Ava has been lulled to sleep, her mouth gaped open, a bit of drool gathering on her chin.

Hawk nods toward the entrance of the tent and we slip out, careful not to wake her, stretching our arms over our heads as we exit. I look at him only to see he's staring at me, stepping slowly toward me with his index finger over his lips.

I back up against the wall as he moves closer, pressing his cheek to mine.

"Hey," he says, his voice a low rumble.

"Hello," I whisper back, almost breathlessly.

"I've been really good this week, you know. Even for a psycho," he says.

"Yes, you have. You've only accosted me at work a few times." I giggle.

"I'm still waiting, though," he says.

"For what?"

Hawk's hands slide up the length of my body then press against my breasts. He cups them firmly, moving his mouth over my ear, nibbling at my earlobe. "To wear you like a straitjacket."

Goosebumps rise all over me, on every exposed piece of skin. I feel butterflies but not in my stomach. *Yes, in my vagina. I have vagina butterflies.*

He slides his hands back down and underneath the edge of my pajama shorts, his fingers gliding over my thighs. "Tell me I can," he begs.

"Yes," I whisper against his skin.

He devours my mouth with his, lapping his tongue against mine and I can smell him—and *god*, he smells so good it makes me crazy. He pulls away and bends down, lifting me over his shoulder and grabbing my ass. I giggle and cover my mouth.

"Shhh, you're gonna get us busted," he says. Hawk fireman-carries me back to his bedroom, setting me down only after he carefully closes the door behind us.

I pull for his shirt as he bends to allow me to tug it all the way off. My hands instinctively rub over the expanse of his chest, then down the rippled muscles of his stomach. He inhales sharply under my touch as he pulls my shirt off in return. My fingertips tease the soft skin atop his boxer briefs before pulling them down along with his shorts.

I step back a few paces and look at him, admire him.

"What are you doing?" he asks, looking down at his own naked body.

"Just filing this memory away for later." I sigh.

"What exactly?" He laughs.

I wave my hand in the air motioning to his entire body and he closes the short distance between us, sweeping me up into his arms and kissing me.

"And you call me psychotic," he says, laughing again. Then, Hawk pushes me back onto his bed and pulls my shorts off. "Roll over," he orders.

Oh. Okay yes. I roll over and prop myself up on my hands and knees, looking back over my shoulder at Hawk. His face is severe, features marbled. I watch him grab a condom and slide it on. Then he slaps my ass and grabs a handful of it, kneading it. He kneels behind me, rubbing himself against my entrance, his hand on my lower back.

"Lean up, honey," he says, wrapping his arm around me and pulling my back against his chest. He brushes my hair to one side, kissing and biting my shoulder, up and down my neck. He bites my earlobe and sucks, blows his hot breath against my wet skin. I moan and press my ass back against him, silently begging for more.

"Drew?" he asks against my cheek.

"Yes?" I exhale.

"I like you," he says.

"I like you, too," I say, breathless, chest heaving.

He slides into me slowly. Every inch of him fills me, making it hard to breathe. His hands wrap around me, cradling my breasts, pinching my nipples and massaging my skin. I moan into the quiet room.

"Shhh," he whispers, rocking our bodies back and forth, pushing into me over and over again.

"I don't think I can," I whisper back, trying hard to stifle the noises mounting in my throat.

"I can help," he says. Hawk covers my mouth with his hand then, careful not to obscure my ability to breathe. He uses this to his advantage, leveraging my head back so I lean into him more.

The pace quickens as he pushes into me over and over again. My moans muffle into the palm of his hand as he bites my clavicle. He finds my clit with two fingers of his free hand and rubs circles over my most sensitive area, sending me spiraling in the most delicious way.

"Come with me," he commands, and I don't let him down.

We collapse after that, tangled around the other, chests heaving, trying hopelessly to catch our breath.

This feeling, this moment, is everything. And I want to fall asleep right here, just like this.

"Don't fall asleep," he whispers, pulling away from me.

"Why?" I ask.

"We have to go back to the fort," he reminds me.

My eyes flutter open. *Ava. Right.*

We crawl back into the fort after we get dressed, right back to our original spots. Sometime while we were gone, Ava kicked her blanket off, and Hawk covers her back up. My tender heart can barely take it. He props himself on his elbow, staring down at her.

"She's a good one," he says.

"Yeah," I say, smiling at her.

He lays his head down on his pillow, looking up at the blankets, but I stare at the two of them a little longer. I don't remember feeling this with Curtis. This excitement, this electricity. Not ever. Not like this. I lie back and stare up at the patterns on the blankets, taking it all in.

This happiness, will it last? Or will it hurt worse because it feels so much bigger? I know it's only just started, but I can't help but think forward. Maybe it's because of Ava, but I'm always trying to think ahead. Be one step ahead of the heartache. I finally fall asleep, sordid thoughts swirling around.

———

MY EYES FLUTTER OPEN IN THE SOFT LIGHT INSIDE THE blanket fort. I turn to see if Ava and Hawk are awake, but they're both still sound asleep. Ava's arm is stretched across Hawk's chest, her head resting on his shoulder. His hand is folded neatly over hers.

They're just lying there, as naturally as two people ever have, like they've been doing it forever. Tears well up in the corners of my eyes. My heart swells and collapses over and over again.

There in the blanket fort, I find myself having a silent panic attack in the early morning hours while my whole world sleeps inches away. I panic.

And then I run away.

CAN'T FEEL MY FACE
HAWK

Correct me if I'm wrong, but when you're in a relationship with someone, you're supposed to actually communicate, right? Maybe a text or two? Maybe a phone call? Smoke signal? But it's Sunday night, and I've gotten nothing. Just crickets. I think she's avoiding me and I'm worried, considering she left in a hurry Saturday morning. Actually, if she'd tried to get out of my door any faster, she would have needed to throw Ava down the stairs.

I tried texting her to make sure everything was okay, to make sure she was home safe at least. And what does she do? She gives me the one-word answer: *Yeah.* Just fucking *yeah*—and that's it. That's all I've gotten out of her all weekend. I tried calling but she freaking pushed the hater button on me. Straight to voicemail like I was a goddamn debt collector. I tried texting her goodnight, asking how Ava was, and crickets.

Listen, I'm not usually that guy, okay? That super clingy stalkerish guy who is freaking out after dating for a week but, this is making me feel like that guy. Even though, I sort of feel justified right now—legit right now—standing in front of her apartment door, uninvited and ready to ask her what the hell is going on.

I lean my forearm against her door frame and knock. After several moments, Drew pulls the door open, her eyes downcast, arm tucked over her middle. I can almost feel how upset she is in the space between us and I try to reach for her but she steps back.

"Drew, what's wrong?" I ask.

"Nothing," she says.

"Right. Well, I don't want to say I don't believe you or anything, but that leaves me in a really difficult position."

"Look, I think we may have started something that was a bad idea," she says, her eyes still on her feet.

"Wait, what?" I stumble back. "Jesus, I thought something happened. I thought you were upset about…I don't know, something else. Not me, though. Not us."

"Listen, you didn't do anything wrong," she starts.

"Oh, what a relief. I didn't do anything wrong, and I'm still getting dumped. That makes it all better." I grimace. "This doesn't make any sense."

"I just don't think getting involved with anyone is a good idea right now," she says.

"Why? Why are you *really* ending this?" I try to keep my voice calm because fuck, we're still in the hallway of her apartment building, but it's getting difficult.

"Because! Because of Ava, okay?" she exclaims.

And I don't understand because I thought Ava and I were great. So I say it. "I don't understand," I say, my voice calmer.

"And you never will, because you're not a parent. But the truth is, she's attached. Too attached. And her own fucking father left her. And if he can do it to her, what makes me think you won't?" she says, venom in her tone.

I swallow hard, because I understand better than she thinks but she doesn't need to hear anything from me right now. And once a mother gets to this place, to these thoughts and feelings, it's hard to argue with her, hard to rationalize anything else.

"Okay," I say, my own eyes trailing down to my feet. My entire body slumps over in defeat.

"I'll look for a new job," she says.

My eyes dart back up but she still won't look at me. "Drew, look at me. Please, look at me," I beg.

Drew's eyes finally find mine. They're red rimmed and glossy.

"You don't have to leave the shop," I say. "Please don't leave the shop. I'm not insane. We're adults. We can exist in the same space."

Her throat moves up and down, her shoulders relaxing. "Okay," she says.

"And Ava can still wait in my apartment. No need for her to be ripped away from her routine," I say.

She nods along, but I can't even tell if she can hear me because she's just staring at a spot on the floor where the carpet is torn.

"I'll see you tomorrow, then," I say. "And Drew?"

"Yeah?" she murmurs.

"Please, if you're in trouble, if you need anything, please know that I'm still here," I say, trying to reassure her.

Then, I walk down the stairs in her building and out into the evening air, exhaling before drawing in a large breath. I think I held it all the way down.

I begin the walk back to my place, quite certain despite telling Drew she could stay at the shop she'll look for another job anyway. Which kills me. I want her and Ava to be okay, to be safe. The thought of them out there in the city, somewhere I can't at least keep an eye on them, frightens the shit out of me.

Will's words echo in mind, around the time Drew was first hired. *You know damn well we take care of our own. As of today, Drew's our own. And that includes Ava.* That was the point of Bird's Eye, really. To build a family.

When I went to Will with the idea of opening my own shop and asked her to help me run it, she left her job at another tattoo shop without a second thought. Somehow, we became a place for misfits. For people who don't have a lot of family to speak of. Or at the very least, for people like me—fatherless and bitter.

A few had come and gone over the years. Avery, though, he stayed. His father was a military man, generous with Avery's discipline and punishment from a young age until it became full blown abuse. His mother left, unable to take his father's wrath anymore. He never blamed her, not for leaving or abandoning him. He just said it was a game of survival.

Hanson came a little while later as an apprentice. Honestly, I don't really know much about the boy. He's almost ten years my junior, has a Brazilian accent the ladies die over, and I think his mother overdosed or his father's in prison or maybe it's both. He doesn't talk about it and we don't ask. It's the rule.

I walk back up the stairs to my place and I want to drink. Or punch something. Or both. As I open my door and step inside, my phone begins to buzz from inside my pocket. I thumb for it eagerly, hoping and praying it's Drew.

Nina: What are you doing?

Me: Come over.

I'm numb anyway. So it won't matter.

GUNS BLAZING
DREW

The week at work has passed quietly. You could've heard a pin drop in here at any given moment. Hawk hasn't spoken to me. We've worked around each other in complete silence. And though I haven't fully explained what's going on to Ava, she knows something's up. Every day she comes in and gets Hawk's apartment key from him and every day she tries to act the way she always has with him. But he's quieter, not all smiles. Every day he grows a little more rigid. Of course, he's still nice to her, but it's different, like he's masking other emotions.

My mind is lost to these thoughts when a large man who's just been tattooed on the neck by Avery appears in front of the counter. He's the size of a fucking linebacker. I'm convinced he could crush my skull with one hand.

"I don't recall seeing you on their website," he says.

First of all, ew. "I'm sorry?" I ask, attempting to remain neutral.

"Under their goods and services menu. I didn't see you listed," he says, grinning to reveal his two front gold-capped teeth.

Okay, second of all, I'm going to throw up in my mouth. "I'm not a good or a service, so…"

"How about I get your number?" he asks.

This man has a tattoo on the side of his face that says *hustle* and every time he speaks it stretches weird and almost looks like it says *turtle,* so I laugh.

"What's so funny?" he asks, his fists clenching at his sides.

"Nothing."

"What, you got a boyfriend or something?" he asks.

I'm acutely aware of other people in the space now, watching this transaction. If I had to guess, I'd say Hawk is definitely somewhere behind me, quietly watching. "No, but—"

"So what's the problem?" he asks, sliding his hand over mine.

I try to pull back but the thing weighs as much as a fucking anvil. "I'm just not interested," I state.

The man scoffs at me—actually scoffs. Like how dare I not reciprocate his interest. He leans in too close to me and I can't move back because there's a fucking hand-vil anchoring me to the counter. His breath smells like cigarettes and maybe whatever he ate for breakfast this morning.

"I could show you a real good time," he says, in nearly a growl.

And it's not sexy. It's not a sexy Hawk growl.

"She said no." Hawk's voice comes from somewhere behind me and I twist to look back at him.

The man eyes Hawk up and down, seemingly unimpressed. "Who are you, her daddy?" He laughs.

Hawk steps toward us, and to my surprise Avery is right behind him, just as square shouldered and with as much intensity in the features of his face. Until now, I've never really noticed how menacing Avery can look. Maybe I never noticed because he seems so easygoing, but here, in this situation, he's just as rigid as Hawk and just as tall.

"No," Hawk says with a laugh. "I'm just a guy who's about two seconds from helping you understand how we treat women in my shop."

The man finally removes his hand from mine and turns his full linebacker body toward Hawk and Avery. *Oh god. Please don't shed blood on my account.*

"You think you can take me?" the man mocks.

"Maybe not," Hawk says, tightening his arms over his chest. "But I'll give it hell."

"And while you're busy with him, you won't see me coming," Avery adds, clenching his jaw.

"And while the two of them might be getting their asses kicked by you, I will definitely choke you out from behind and feel your body grow limp in my arms," Hanson says, appearing from the back hall, arms outstretched like the coming messiah.

Hanson is young, the youngest here. He's also not as muscular, more lean, like a swimmer. But his threat, the tone of it, both sinister and playful, spoken in his accent, is probably one of the most frightening things I've ever heard.

"And when they're done, and your body's laying limp on the floor, I'm going to make them tattoo a fucking dick on your forehead, you piece of shit," a small voice says behind the men, but it travels over the entire scene.

This little piece of poetry comes from Will's mouth. She walks over and stands beside me, slinging one arm around me and putting her hand on her jutted out hip.

The big man finally takes a step back. "Whatever," he says.

"Right, well, you should probably just pay now, and then you need to find somewhere else to get your work done," Avery says.

The man throws a wad of cash on the counter and walks out, mumbling and cussing under his breath.

I look back at all of them, my eyes roaming from one to the next. The men of Bird's Eye. Even Will, who once told me she feels like a man in the shop too, because they don't even register that she has tits. They're all watching to make sure he's not coming back.

Will turns to me. "Are you okay?" she asks.

"Yeah, I'm fine," I say, finally exhaling.

"Don't worry, girl. We've got you," Hanson says, winking at me, his playful sinister smile still plastered on his face.

I look at Hawk, and his face is not playful. There's no smile detected. He quietly turns and walks back to his booth, where he collects his belongings, and then heads out the back door.

"Oh shit," I say. "Is he mad at me?"

"Fuck no," Avery says. He clasps his hands on my shoulder. "He would never be mad at you for something like that."

"Hey, why don't I come over tonight and bring wine?" Will cuts in, diverting my attention.

I nod, because Will and wine sound good. Really fucking good.

"Great," she says. "I'll text you." Then she disappears out the back door too.

I walk to the back to collect my purse and jacket, stopping in front of the stock room to catch my breath. I can feel dampness on my cheeks. I didn't even realize I was crying. Soft, silent tears stream down.

"Oh, honey, what's wrong?" Hanson asks. His long arms wrap

around me and it's not romantic. It's brotherly. Or at least I think this is what it would be like if I had a brother.

Suddenly, a thought splits me open. *Maybe I do have a brother.* And a sister. And another brother. And a...whatever Hawk is. Maybe they really are a family. And I'm part of it.

I sob into Hanson's chest and he strokes my hair. He doesn't ask me any more questions because even in his youth, I think he knows.

Walking the path of denial is a difficult one.

DON'T LET ME DOWN
HAWK

Granted, storming out of the shop wasn't the best option after that guy pissed me off. But it was either storm out or run after him and pound his face in. Or grab Drew and shake her and tell her to wake up and let me back in. So storming out seemed like the least severe choice in the moment.

Will chased after me and tried to talk some sense into me, calming me down. I was glad she was going to hang out with Drew tonight. That Drew wouldn't be alone. And in an effort not to wallow in loneliness myself, I invited Avery and Hanson over, who should be here any minute.

I finish changing into basketball shorts, thoughts of throttling a man the size of a mountain still swirling in my mind, when I hear them inside. Serves me right after giving them a key for emergencies.

"I see you've made yourselves at home," I say, walking out into the kitchen to see Hanson stuffing his face with chips and salsa.

Avery's face emerges from the fridge and he pops the top from a beer.

"It was a refreshment emergency," Avery says, taking a swig from the glass beer bottle in his hand.

"And a chip emergency," Hanson adds.

I roll my eyes and sit at the bar. "Pass me one," I say to Avery.

He hands me a bottle and I take a long draw from it, savoring the taste, wishing I could drink about twenty. *Because drinking is supposed to make me feel better, right?*

"You're sad, dude," Hanson says.

"Nah," I say, waving him off.

"Yeah, man. You are," Avery says.

I shrug my shoulders. Between the two of them, their most serious relationship was Avery's ex-girlfriend, Kimberly, from three years ago and they lasted a whopping six weeks. Their combined roster totals too many women to count. I think the term is *man whore,* although I never subscribe to societal terms as long as everyone is consenting and having fun.

"No offense, but what do you know about being sad over a woman?" I ask them.

"Ah, my man, just because I've never felt the ache doesn't mean I don't recognize it," Hanson says.

I swear to god, sometimes when he speaks, it's like he's older than me. Maybe it's the accent, I'm not quite sure. He has a mysterious otherworldliness about him.

He places his hand over his heart, like he can feel that ache he mentioned.

"It doesn't matter. It's not a big deal. It was only a week," I lie.

"What the fuck does the length of time have to do with anything?" Avery asks.

"Um, everything?" I offer, quirking my brow.

Avery crosses his arms over his chest and says, "Explain."

"Look, it's not like we were that deep into this thing. Drew and I, we were just getting going. Backing out now, if that's the choice she wants to make, I'm just saying better now than later. Now's less painful. Now's not a big deal."

"Says the guy practically salting his beer." Avery looks at Hanson, pointing his thumb at me, and Hanson nods vigorously with a mouthful of chips.

"I'm not saying it didn't sting. I'm just saying it's fine," I say.

Both men shrug at me and lull into a different conversation, seemingly bored with my denial of what they assume to be a grander situation. But they're wrong. *Aren't they?* A week of dating isn't a long time. Certainly not long enough to be crying into my Wheaties. Or beer.

Maybe it's the loss of potential that's fucking me up. The blowing out of flames before they've had a chance to consume us.

I take my beer over to the couch and sit, throwing my head back. Raven jumps up and nudges my hand until I pet her. I let my mind spiral, thoughts of Drew and Ava flooding everything. I think I miss that kid. Which is weird. Because I've never dated anyone with a kid. I didn't even think I wanted kids of my own. But Ava is cool, and sweet. So easy to like.

"No offense, man, I like hanging out with you—whenever, all the time—but what the hell are you doing?" Avery asks.

"What do you mean?"

"Drew's divorced, right? he asks.

I nod. "What's your point?"

"And the one man who vowed to be there for her no matter what, walked out? Like sickness, health, till death? Just up and poof? Changed his mind?" Avery says, leading me someplace I haven't figured out the destination of yet.

"Yeah, again, what's your point?" I ask.

"So, my point is, right now is the exact moment she needs a guy *not* to run. From anything. No matter what she throws at you, she needs to know you're gonna be there, ready to fight for her and Ava. At least that's how I see it," Avery says. He shrugs his shoulders like it's the most obvious conclusion.

And the more I consider his words...*maybe it is?* "Even when she flat out rejected me?"

Avery's forehead crinkles as he gives this some thought. "Let me ask you a question. Did she actually reject you? Like, did she look at you and say you were ugly? A piece of shit? Not good enough for her or Ava? Did she tell you that you were shit in the sack?" he asks.

"Well, no," I reply.

"Or, did she just get scared?" he muses.

Fucking fuck. "Probably the second thing," I admit.

"And what do you think she needs in order to feel safe? Secure? Not scared? Given what she's been through?" he asks, nodding me along.

"Someone to fight for her?" I guess.

"She needs a goddamn man to show up. Every single time, dude. No matter what. Show the fuck up," Avery says. With that, he takes a sip of his beer.

Goddammit. My phone buzzes in my pocket and I pull it out, seeing a notification from Will. I push it open to see a picture message. Drew is sitting on the ugly green couch, eyes downcast, staring into her glass of wine. She looks so sad I wish I could reach through the phone and caress her cheek.

Double goddammit.

TO BE SO LONELY
DREW

The wine doesn't taste quite as sweet tonight. Luckily, Ava went to bed early because I've been close to sobbing every five minutes ever since Will got here. I take another sip of my bitter wine and wonder if it's the wine or me but I already know the answer to that. I think about what Hawk is doing, despite myself. I even have a momentary lapse in judgment and think about texting him. I know Will has been talking to him and I fight the urge to ask her what he's doing, how he is.

"How much longer will I be experiencing this mope?" she asks.

I let out a long sigh and finish the wine in my glass. "I can't say for sure."

"There's a cure, you know," she says, and I look at her. "He's about six-four, lots of tattoos. Some might say he has a devastating jaw…"

"You don't think so?" I ask.

"Ew, no. I look at Hawk the way you look at Hanson," she

says. Then she waves her hand over her crotch. "Zip. Nada. Nothing."

I laugh, even in my current state. "Come on. The entire time you've known him? Not even once?"

"Not even once." She shakes her head, sticking out her tongue in disgust. "Sure, I mean, I get why others think he's dreamy, but it's just a no for me."

I can't fathom knowing Hawk my entire life and not getting the vagina butterflies a single time. Knowing someone that long...you know they've seen each other at least mostly naked at some point. Her loss is my gain. Rather, was my gain. Not so much anymore.

"Who's had your heart all these years, then? Anyone?" I ask, eager to change the topic.

Will shifts uncomfortably for the first time possibly ever and tucks her hair behind her ear. "I haven't dated anyone in a while. My last boyfriend was a dick."

"Right...but that's not what I asked." I raise an eyebrow at her because there's definitely something here and I'm not letting her off that easy.

She shifts again and sips her wine. "Fine! Okay, yeah. Of course there's a guy. I've known him a really long time. But we're pretty different and he would never go for someone like me."

"Someone like you? He's not into badass women? Awesome, funny, smart women?" I ask.

"You wouldn't understand," she says.

"Well, have you told him?"

"God no!" she yelps.

"So then how do you know? Hawk and I are pretty different, and you were all for it," I point out.

"Yeah, and look how that turned out," she scoffs.

Ouch. But also, fair point. Still, I wince.

"I'm sorry," she says.

"No, that's fair," I tell her, nodding.

"Still doesn't mean I should've said it," she says. "It's just... he and I, I don't think we'd work. I don't think he sees me like that. Then again, I'm starting to think no man sees me like that. I'm in a perpetual state of being *one of the guys*." She inhales and exhales a long deep breath, a sense of hopelessness swallowing up her features.

I just can't believe this about men. Can they not see how adorable she is? How awesome? She's truly the best and deserves the best. For a moment, I wonder if it's her tattoos, but there are plenty of tattooed women who are regularly worshipped. And dammit, Will should be one of them. She's impressive. Very impressive.

Her parents are the type of religious who are not accepting or tolerant, though. So as soon as she turned to tattoos and something other than the Christian rock radio station, they started preaching and praying and begging her to put down her wicked ways, to cast out the devil. Considering this, she doesn't exactly have any *parents* to speak of. She calls them Marty and Susan. Which is why she hates it when Hawk uses her middle name—Susan, after her mother.

"I think the right man will," I say.

Will smiles at my answer, a hint of hesitant hope playing across her features. Her phone buzzes in her hand and despite my winning streak, I can't help myself any longer.

"What's he doing?" I ask.

"He had the guys come over for drinks," she says.

"And how is he?"

"About as miserable as you are," she says, tilting her head at me.

I stare off at a spot on the wall for a minute and she goes on.

"Did he ever tell you about Rick?" she asks.

I search my mind for anyone named Rick in any stories he's told me and come up empty. "I don't think so?"

"Doesn't surprise me," she says, sitting up a little straighter and leaning in toward me. "Look, maybe I shouldn't tell you this, but he told me what you said to him, okay? That day when he came here. How you thought he might do what your ex did, or at least could be capable of it. And how he'd never understand. So you need to know about Rick."

I sit up and lean in toward her too, like we're sharing a secret. Maybe because in a way we are. I nod for her to go on.

"Rick was his stepdad for a short time. Well, as close as he ever got to one. His mom dated this guy for a little while. Anyway, Rick was the best. Took him places, bought him stuff, was totally nice to him and his brother Derek. We were in the sixth grade, then. Then one day Hawk went home, and the guy was just gone," she says, shrugging her shoulders.

"Are you serious?" I say, my mouth falling open.

"His mom was sitting at the table crying. The dude told her he couldn't handle the pressure of being a dad to someone else's kids or something like that, and just split," Will says, looking me straight in the eye. "So yeah, Hawk gets it. Hawk knows exactly how a man can hurt a family, father or not."

I lean back on the arm of the couch slowly, taking this new information in, turning it over in my mind.

"You wanna see for yourself?" She holds up her phone before tossing it into my lap.

"Oh my god, no. I couldn't do that," I say, attempting to shove it back to her.

"Look, he'll tell *you* whatever you ask him. But it seems like *you* have a problem asking him. So just think of it like you get to ask what you need with a little identity protection," she suggests.

"I don't know," I say, staring down at the screen of her phone.

"Suit yourself." She holds her hand out but I grip her phone, reluctant to hand it over, and she sits back. "That's what I thought," she says, smirking in all her fucking wisdom.

I open her texts with him and scroll up, looking at a couple of their most recent ones. She hasn't asked him much and he hasn't offered much so I scroll up more. "Oh my god, you sent him a picture of me?"

Will simply shrugs her shoulders and points at the phone. Underneath the photo is his response.

Hawk: How is she?

Will: Sad.

Hawk: Me too.

Will: You guys are dumb.

Hawk: I'm trying to give her what she wants.

Will: You're even more dumb for thinking that.

Hawk: People here seem to agree with you.

I hover over the keyboard, trying to think about what to say, what to ask. For whatever reason, my thoughts circle around to Curtis in our final months, what I might have asked him, how I might have approached him.

Me (as Will): Do you miss her?

Hawk: Duh.

Me: Why don't you just call up one of those girls who give you their number? Plenty to choose from.

Hawk: Who are you even talking to right now? Gross.

Me: I'm just saying. It's not like it was a big deal.

Hawk: Don't say that.

Me: What?

Hawk: It was important to me.

Me: Do you want another pic of her?

Hawk: Yes. Does that make me a creep?

Me: Maybe.

I hand the phone back to Will, who scrolls through the brief messages I exchanged in her place.

"Oh shit, strike a pose," she says.

I awkwardly try to put my elbow in four different places. I'm sure nothing I am currently doing looks natural or normal.

"Okay, you're terrible at this," she says. She reaches over and moves my body parts for me. "Now, look over at me but like you're not expecting me to be taking a picture, like I caught you off guard," she encourages.

This is so stupid. What are we, in middle school? I try to act surprised and we retake the photo three times before she's satisfied with my fake surprised face. She hits send and we don't have to wait long.

Hawk. Beautiful.

Hawk: This is dumb.

Hawk. I'm coming over.

PLAYING FOR KEEPS
HAWK

I'm walking as fast as my slightly drunken legs can carry me to Drew's apartment. I wish I was sober so I could've driven and been there faster, but this wasn't exactly planned. And because I'm making my *big move* as Hanson called it, he and Avery are walking with me.

"This is it, man," Hanson says.

"Yeah, dude. This is gonna work," Avery says.

They're hyping me up and I don't know if it's working or making me want to puke. I notice in my inebriated state that they say *dude* and *man* a fucking lot, too.

We round the corner and I break into a near sprint to her building, stopping just shy of the front door, catching my breath as the guys jog to catch up.

"Dude, nobody runs while they're drunk," Avery says.

"Yeah, dude. Not cool," Hanson says, placing his hands on his knees and breathing hard.

I head inside, where I take the stairs two at a time with the guys on my heels, and then I knock on her apartment door. I wait for half a second and knock again.

Will opens the door, swaying side to side a little. "He's here," she calls over her shoulder.

Drew bounces down the small hallway to the front door, her eyes on me at first before catching the sight of Avery and Hanson right behind me.

"Drew," I say. "Please, I need to talk to you."

"Oh god, everyone's here? Come in," she says, motioning for us all to pile in, and now I realize we're going to have an entire goddamn half-drunken audience for this.

The five of us stand in the small living room, awkwardly staring at one another. Everyone involved is clearly unsure what to do next.

"Oh for fuck's sake, will one of you goobers give me a ride home?" Will asks Avery and Hanson.

"No can do, my lady. But we can give you a walk home?" Hanson offers, laughing.

"A walk home?" she repeats.

"We walked here with Hawk," Avery says, and Will rolls her eyes.

"How about a piggyback ride?" Hanson asks.

"So your drunk ass can drop me?" she counters.

I put a stop to the disaster by telling them to walk back to my place and look after Raven and Sadie for me, telling them they can crash there until morning. Whether I'm back tonight or not, that's a good plan. And it works. They walk out of the apartment, while Hanson's still swearing he's coherent enough to piggyback Will the entire way.

Then there were two. Drew and I stand frozen, my hands stuffed in my pockets, because if I take them out I'll want to touch her and I don't think that's the right thing to do.

"Do you want something to drink?" she offers, to which I swallow hard and nod. She motions to the couch, so I sit as she disappears into the kitchen.

My grip tightens on the edge of the cushion because the entire way over here, this isn't how I planned this in my mind. I was going to come in, swoop her up, kiss her, woo her. I was going to be bold. Now I'm sitting on the itchy couch and she's handing me a glass of water. I take a big gulp because suddenly my mouth is dry.

"What are you doing here, Hawk?" she asks.

Now's my chance. It's now or never. Do or die. Win or don't. *What? Shut up.* I turn to Drew, her eyes fixed on my face, features unreadable. *Is that hope? Fear? Both?*

"I came to tell you I'm not going anywhere," I say.

She tilts her head, confused by my words.

"I came to tell you I know you're scared and I know you think I might bail, but I'm not. I'm going to be here—right here, every day. Maybe we won't last, okay? Maybe down the road we break up, but it won't be because I suddenly disappeared, because I suddenly stopped showing up. I can promise you that. And I know you shouldn't give up on us for fear of that before we even try."

I let silence fall over the room. I let her chew on my words while I await her response.

"How do you know you won't disappear?" she asks.

I wince. "You've had it done to you before, right? Would you ever do that to someone?" I ask.

She shakes her head, adamantly.

"Yeah, well, so have I. I've been on the receiving end. It makes me physically ill to think about doing that. Especially to you and Ava," I say.

A small smile begins to play on her lips. The first one I've seen from her all week. Drew scoots closer to me on the couch, her legs almost touching mine, and I can feel the heat from her skin.

"You promise?" she asks.

"I will show up for you and Ava every day," I say. "I promise."

Drew leans up, lifting one leg over me to straddle me before she sinks onto my lap. My hands instinctively reach up inside the back of her shirt, caressing the bare skin of her back and god I've missed her warmth.

She leans in closer to me, pressing her forehead to mine, inhaling. "I missed you."

"I missed you too, straitjacket," I whisper, then I grip her tight and pull her even closer to me, listening to her giggle.

Then, I take her mouth with mine. I kiss her for the first time in too long. I devour, suck, taste. I lap my tongue against hers, hungry with need. I can't stop myself. I kiss her breathless, clawing at her clothes and skin. I reach down the front of her pants and discover she isn't wearing any panties.

"Oh my," I say against her mouth. I rub my fingers against her, pulling my kiss away to muffle her whimpers with my hand. Her fingers grip my biceps and I feel her nails start to dig into my skin. "Do you like that?" I ask.

She nods, arching her body against me.

"Do you want more?" I ask.

She grips me tighter, nodding again.

I guide her hand to my pants so she can unzip me while I keep rubbing against her, but she stops just as she exposes me, moving my palm from her mouth.

"Wait, I don't have any condoms here," she says.

I reach into my pants pocket and pull one out. "I guess you could say I was hopeful," I whisper.

She laughs again as I roll it on.

As she stands to take her pants off, I grab her ass and shove my mouth between her legs, desperate to taste her because she tastes so fucking good. She moans too loudly and covers her own mouth, using her free hand to grab a handful of my hair, guiding me the way she likes it.

She pushes me back and returns to her straddling position, pulling my shirt off and then hers, so our bare chests can touch. Her soft, warm skin presses against mine as I wrap my arms around her, guiding her up and down my length over and over again. I push into her as deep as I can go, feeling her body shudder.

She kisses my lips and bites my jaw, moving down my throat, and then bites into my collarbone. She pulses against me and I pull back on her hair, exposing her throat and breasts to my mouth. I gently kiss the ink of the tattoo I gave her, nearly healed. I kiss down the tops of her tits, putting her nipples in my mouth one at a time, sucking and nibbling.

She feels so good, I can't get enough of her. I don't want this to end but I can't slow it down. It's a frenzy. I find solace in knowing I'll have more of these moments with her, more time with her—getting to know her, exploring her body and her mind. I am desperate to know everything, ask everything.

We finish and I put my shorts back on. Then, I spoon her on the itchy green couch, because to my dismay this is where Drew sleeps.

"We have to get you a proper bed, babe."

She laughs. "I'm working on it."

"And a less itchy couch," I suggest.

"I don't have the money for that," she says.

"Okay, when is your birthday?"

She laughs again. "You're not getting me furniture for my birthday."

"I can't spend the night with you like this," I say. "And I want to. So really, it's a completely greedy gesture."

"Okay, you can get me a bed. But *just* a bed. Like, the cheapest bed you can find."

"Umm, I have a bad back. I'm old. I need a fancy mattress, great sheets, memory foam, the works. Don't worry, I'll take care of it," I say, patting her on the head.

She laughs, because I think she knows I'm serious and there's nothing she can do to stop me now.

"But really, when is your birthday?" I ask again.

"February fifth. Yours?"

"June seventeenth," I say.

"I guess I'll have to think of what to get you," she says.

"You. Wearing a bow. Just a bow. Nothing else. A sexy, slutty bow," I say.

Her laughter fills the quiet apartment, echoing down the hall, and I cover her mouth.

"Okay, you know what, if we get caught at any point, it's definitely going to be your fault," I say.

We fall into sleepy, comfortable conversation, trading questions back and forth. Some silly, some meaningful. Our favorite
things, facts about ourselves, more family stuff. Eventually, Drew
drifts to sleep in my arms. I hold her tight, desperate for her
closeness, for her touch. I don't know what's happening, how I
got here, or what I'm feeling. I just know it feels good and right.

WHAT I WOULDN'T DO
DREW

I wake up, still curled up with Hawk on this godforsaken couch with a crick in my neck because fuck this godforsaken couch. Though, I don't care quite as much as I normally would, given the *curled up with Hawk* part. I make every attempt to quietly roll over and face him but I nearly fall off the couch. The only thing saving me is his grip.

"What are you doing?" he sleepily mumbles.

"Sorry, did I wake you?" I whisper.

"Yes, you woke me. But it's okay. Being awake with you is better than dreaming of you. Although you were wearing a slutty nurse's uniform in my dream," he says, opening one eye as a big sleepy grin spreads across his perfect lips.

"I was *what?*" I say in a hushed tone.

"Maybe something to put on the list for Halloween suggestions." He shrugs and pulls me close.

Just then we hear a bedroom door open and Ava appears in the hallway. We both freeze.

"Do you think if we're very still, she won't see us? Like a T. Rex?" he whispers in my ear.

Despite the joke, and my giggle, his lips against my ear send a shiver down my spine.

"Hawk?" Ava says.

Hawk pokes his head up from behind me, looking sheepish, and a tad concerned. "Yeah, kid, it's me. Who else would it be?"

"Yay!" Ava says, bounding across the living room and jumping onto us, creating a dog pile of people.

Ava and Hawk go at it, exchanging fake punches, and then he tickles her belly and messes up her hair. After she tries to straighten it, she asks for breakfast and uses me as a human slide to slither off the couch and into the kitchen.

"I'll cook," Hawk offers, unwrapping himself from me.

The empty spot on the couch behind me now makes my skin feel cold, and I tuck myself into the blankets as I listen to Ava tell Hawk all about her entire week at school since she hadn't been able to do that in as much detail as of late.

I close my eyes and listen to their conversation. It sounds so natural, so at ease, and I'm still getting used to it.

"Babe?" Hawk yells from the kitchen, pulling me from my thoughts.

"Yeah?"

"Where are your spatulas? Where are your pans? I'm lost," he says.

I laugh, knowing he's probably not lost but just can't find the only ones we have. I get up and head to the kitchen, where I pull out the one spatula and pan that exist in the entire apartment and hand them to him.

He looks at them, confusion twisting his features. Soon, they soften. "That's it," he says. "You can protest all you want. You can kick and scream. But we're going shopping today. You can't live like this. This is barbaric," he says.

The way the words fall from his mouth aren't to embarrass me. He knows the deal with the apartment, that nothing here is mine. His comedic tone makes me laugh.

"You really don't have to do that," I say.

He puts the pan and spatula down on the counter and cradles my face with his giant hands. "Listen, I know I don't have to or need to. I know you're strong and eventually would do all this yourself anyway. But I want to come visit you. And this tiny fucking pan isn't even going to hold enough eggs for all of us." He laughs, then leans in close to whisper, "And that couch is going to make my back so sore, I can't make the sex with you."

I giggle again as he laughs into my neck. I hug him tight, not wanting to relinquish so much control or feel dependent so soon but also knowing that isn't how he means it. "Okay. I guess we can go shopping for a few things."

"Yeah," he says. "A few." His eyebrows are raised on his forehead in such a way that something tells me his *few* and my *few* are two very different things.

———

HAVE YOU EVER BEEN TO IKEA ON A WEEKEND? NEVER go. It's the worst. But if you go, get the meatballs. Because yum. Ava and Hawk shovel the meatballs into their mouths almost simultaneously as he watches me pick a new spatula.

"Get more than one," he says, waving me back to the rack. "Get a few different kinds."

I put three spatulas in the cart, along with several cooking spoons, tongs, dish towels, and a brand new set of approximately twenty pots and pans. Even though I tell him I don't think that many are necessary, he insists. I don't put up much of a fight though, because they're copper and pretty.

Hawk puts a set of glasses in the cart next and tells me we're throwing out all the ones that don't match. He also adds fancy salt and pepper shakers, and other random kitchen contraptions I've never seen.

We meander through the bathroom section and pause as he starts to grab towels. "We said a *few* things," I remind him.

"Okay, well what's your towel situation?" he asks.

"I mean, we have some?" I stare back.

"Are they big enough to go around me?" he asks, motioning down his body.

I take the moment to assault him with my eyes, sweeping up and down his torso, across his chest.

"That's what I thought," he says.

He places matching fluffy bath towels, hand towels, a floor mat, and matching shower curtain in the cart.

I roll my eyes at him, smirking. "Do you just like spending all your money?"

He smirks back, nodding and pointing in direction of the couches. "So, a couch then?"

Ava jumps onto the cart, hanging on for dear life as Hawk navigates it through the aisles and around the other patrons.

The two of them play in the fake kitchens, and they also insist on sitting on every single couch in the place before we choose one. In their words, the new one has to be *non-itchy*, so it's important to make sure first.

We also pick out a kitchen table set, because Hawk makes the point that the three of us can't even sit down to eat at the one I currently have, and I can't argue with that logic.

One cart becomes two, at some point. *Yes, we have two fucking carts now.* I'm almost embarrassed but it's so hard to feel anything but good and special and unconcerned with anyone else's opinions when Hawk's around.

He walks through the crowd with such confidence. People stare at him for different reasons. Half of them are in awe of his beauty, the other half are probably intimidated. I assume some stare because of the tattoos, others because of his size. Either way, they all part like the Red Sea, like he's some kind of tattooed, blue eyed messiah.

Ava and I walk with him on this venture, but while she's completely oblivious, I'm completely aware of the eyes on me holding his hand.

"Okay, I think we're done?" I finally ask.

"We need one more thing," he says. We navigate the store until we're surrounded by youthful pink fluffy stuff.

"Ava?" he says.

"Yeah?" she says, arching her neck all the way back to look up at him.

Hawk crosses his arms over his chest and smiles. "Pick a bed, and all the things that go with it."

Ava's face lights up brighter than I've seen in some time and she takes off running, trying bed after bed to decide which she likes best.

Watching her choose a bed is better than anything else thus far in my opinion. The happiness she's feeling right now is unmatched, and it's all I need to feel content.

Eventually, we check out and go, with the Jeep filled to the brim with most of the small stuff and a slip of paper with a delivery date for the rest. In two business days, my apartment will be completely transformed, and I have Hawk to thank for that.

I think in any other way with any other person, this might've felt strange. Like charity, or a hand out. Somehow, Hawk makes it feel nice. Like I'm being pampered, spoiled. It's a strange feeling, but something tells me I should get used to it.

After he drops us off back at the apartment, I lie on the itchy green couch for one of the last times and my phone buzzes in my pocket. I take it out and realize I have a voicemail from my Aunt Penny, which is strange because I haven't heard from her since she left.

I play the voicemail, but it's all muffled and broken up. I can barely make out what she says, as every other word or so is cut off by the static.

Well, that doesn't help. I hit the button to call her back but it rings until I get her voicemail, which is full. *Of course.* I don't think she even knows how to delete them.

I shrug, deciding I'll try again tomorrow. My phone buzzes in my hand again but this time, it's a text from Hawk.

Hawk: I just got to my apartment. It's quiet and empty and I don't like it.

Me: Raven and Sadie are there.

Hawk: Ok fair. Let me try again. I just got to my apartment. It's empty of your presence and absent of Ava's laugh and I don't like it.

I swear to god, my heart just falls out onto the floor and flops around right then and there.

Me: I miss you too.

Hawk: Can I take you guys somewhere this week? After work?

Me: Yeah, where?

Hawk: You know I'm not going to tell you.

Me: Okay, psycho.

I press my phone to my chest, because yeah, maybe he's a little psycho. Maybe he looks a little menacing, a little sinister. Some might even say dangerous.

But that's okay. Because he's *my* psycho.

YOU PICKED ME
DREW

I t's early afternoon, and I'm at the front counter. Hawk
offered to wait at my apartment for the IKEA delivery and
set it all up. Since he didn't have any appointments today,
it made more sense. They always give you one of those really
vague delivery windows equivalent to *we'll be there between the ass
crack of dawn and dinner time,* so I was happy he was able to do it.
He also offered to handle getting rid of the old stuff while he
waited.

Man things. That's what I call that stuff. He's doing man things
for me.

I'm restocking the merchandise cases in the front, occasionally watching Hanson work on someone's forearm when I hear
the bell sound over the door. I turn to greet the person, momentarily thrown off by who it is, but I put on my best poker face
because *WHAT THE FUCK?*

"Hi, can I help you?" I ask her.

Her annoying bright red hair falls over the paw prints on her chest. *Nina*. Hawk's ex-girlfriend. The very sight of her makes my eyes hurt, but I plaster on my best fake smile.

"Is Hawk here?" she asks, snapping her gum, adjusting the Coach purse she has in the crook of her arm. She twirls one of her discolored hair extensions with her long fake fingernails.

What the fuck did Hawk see in her? Or am I just the most boring person he's ever dated? Am I super boring? I'm still comparing myself to her when I answer.

"No, he's not in right now," I say. "But I can give him a message if you need me to?" I make the offer just to play nice, knowing she has his number, knowing she can just handle it herself.

She huffs loudly, as if she's annoyed at this inconvenience. "I think I forgot my jacket at his place last week. I'll just text him later."

Her mouth keeps moving but I don't hear anything after the first two sentences she spits out. She puts on her annoyingly large sunglasses and leaves, and everything feels really fuzzy and far away. *Is this what a panic attack feels like?*

I run to the back and stuff myself into the stock room, not sure what else to do. I don't want to text him about it—that would be terrible. I can't leave work because Ava will be here soon. And I can't exactly make it there, accuse him of cheating, and make it back in time to get her. Plus, I'll likely be a blubbering mess when he confesses and just want to ball up in the bottom of the bathtub with ice cream and wine.

Okay, wait. Get ahold of yourself. Technically he didn't cheat. I ended things. So…he just hooked up with Nina while we were apart. *Jesus. Nina? Why her? Why did it have to be her?* I have to push these thoughts aside until I can accuse him—I mean *ask* him about what happened.

I smooth my hands over my shirt and emerge from the stock room, trying hard to keep my breathing steady.

For the next hour or so until Ava arrives from school, I go into autopilot mode and zone out. Even after she arrives, I can only half-hear her talking about a boy at recess and her friend during science. I need to get out of here. I need to haul ass to my apartment. I need to punch Hawk. *No. Calm down. You don't know, Drew. You don't know. Stay positive.*

But why the hell else would her jacket be there? And where the fuck is it? Under his bed?

Oh my god, no. Stop. Calm down.

I watch the clock for the last fifteen minutes of my shift and grab Ava's hand at the exact moment it's time to go, gliding out the door without even saying goodbye to anyone.

One way or another, I will have answers.

———

WHEN I MAKE IT TO THE APARTMENT PARKING LOT, I notice the itchy green couch sticking out of the dumpster. How he got it down the stairs and in there is a mystery to me. I step closer and notice nearly everything from the apartment is in there. The futon, the wobbly stool, the one good chair.

I pull Ava inside and up the stairs and open the apartment door, fully expecting to walk into an empty space because Hawk didn't say anything about the new stuff having been delivered when we texted today. But it's not empty. Not even close.

We round the corner to see the beautiful navy colored sofa I picked out in place of where the green one had been. Underneath the window, he's sneakily added a matching navy chair. Mustard yellow throw pillows sit on both pieces of furniture.

My feet hit a plush area rug and I definitely don't remember picking that out, or the pillows. *Did he get this stuff when I wasn't looking?* I hear him in the kitchen and I cross the floor, my eyes fixed toward where the noise is coming from.

The small dining set I chose is under the window, adorned with place mats and a vase of flowers. I can seat four people now. I turn to see Hawk putting away glasses in the cabinet.

"Hey! You're here," he says, excitement hanging on every word.

"Hawk, this place looks incredible," I say, still looking around, taking it all in.

I see the fancy salt and pepper shakers we picked out, sitting on the kitchen counter next to a brand new toaster and electric can opener.

"This is way more than I picked out," I say.

His movements pause as he looks at me. "I may have gone back. I may have also realized some things were missing when I started setting up," he says, looking around nervously. "Are you mad?"

"I don't think so," I say, running my finger over the copper pots he hasn't put away yet.

He laughs. "Go check out the rest while I put these away," he says, smiling and nodding toward the bathroom and bedrooms.

Ava and I peer into the bathroom, the matching navy floor mat and shower curtain perfectly in place. A small shelf now hangs over the wall above the toilet, holding bath and hand towels. We look at each other, shock on our faces.

"Oh my god, my bedroom!" she yells.

"Don't you think we should wait for Hawk?" I ask.

Ava runs back to the kitchen and drags Hawk to where I'm standing in front of her bedroom door.

"Go ahead," I say, taking his hand in mine.

Ava opens the door and squeals. On the far side of the room, the white bed she picked is set up with the purple bedding and faux fur pillows. The matching white dresser is on the wall next to us, with a small television on top. Framed posters of classic artwork line the walls and Ava stops and stares at each one. The matching white drawing desk she pointed out sits in the corner next to the window, fully stocked with paper, pencils, colors pencils, and who knows what else.

"I think she'll be in here for the rest of the night," I say, laughing.

Ava flies around the room, touching everything, taking it all in.

"Are you ready to see yours?" Hawk asks me.

"Hawk," I say. "You didn't. I thought we only picked out a bed?"

He steps back, giving way to the other bedroom door. "I guess you'll have to see." The look on his face is complete mischief.

Placing my hand on the doorknob, I suck in a breath, preparing myself for the surprise. I push it open, revealing a completely decorated room. The queen-size bed sits on the far wall, adorned with crisp white linens. Two gold metal side tables with glass tops hug either side, both with small lamps on top. A wide black dresser with a large mirror on top is to my right, across from the bed. A vase of fresh roses on top, next to a small gift box with red ribbon.

"That's for you," he says.

"More?" I ask.

"Just one more." He shrugs, smiling.

The pads of my fingers run over the silky ribbon before pulling them loose. Inside, there's a delicate gold necklace with a diamond pendant. "Hawk, no. This is too much," I say. Even as the words leave my mouth, I'm pulling the necklace out, running my fingers over it.

"Consider it a bonus," he says. "Do you like it?"

"I love it." I walk back over to him, wrapping my arms around his waist, hugging him as tightly as I can.

His arms come around me, his embrace enveloping me. "I just want you and Ava to be good and safe and comfortable," he whispers against the hair on top of my head.

"We are," I say, melting into him. "Thanks to you."

SABOTAGE
HAWK

I'm enjoying this hug, the sweet embrace Drew and I are having in the doorway of *her* bedroom, when suddenly, she pushes away from me.

"Wait," she says, pushing me in the chest further into the room and closing the door behind us. *Oh okay, a little making out, maybe?* Ava's not going to come looking for us. She's way too enthralled in her new space.

"I just remembered I'm mad at you," she exclaims.

Wait, what? "Why?" I ask, watching her fold her arms across her chest.

"I can't even believe you would sit and pretend to care so much about me ending things with you last week when you immediately ran into the arms of another woman," she spits.

"I did fucking *what*?" I ask, blinking several times.

"Nina was at the shop today," she says, like that's supposed to explain everything.

"What does that have to do with anything?"

"Oh, please. She's the woman you ran to, Hawk."

Okay, now I know we're in an alternate reality or something. I'm being Punk'd or some shit. I take a deep breath, clearly not understanding what the hell is happening.

"I'm sorry but you're going to have to spell this out for me, Drew. I'm not following," I say.

"I just can't believe that the moment I have a little doubt about us you get into bed with that Picasso painting," she says.

And I know I shouldn't have done it, but I laugh. Really hard and really loud. "First of all, I'm going to skip over the fact that you called ending things with me *a little doubt* and second, calling Nina a Picasso painting is the best shit I've ever heard. But also, I didn't fucking sleep with her and I'm kind of insulted that you think so," I say.

"Well, when she came by the shop today she said she thinks she left her jacket at your place," Drew says, tapping her foot at me.

"Are you really tapping your foot at me right now?" I say, crossing my arms over my chest.

She doesn't say anything but her eyes start to tear up and *oh god no*. She really thinks something happened.

"Please come here," I say, reaching for her hand, guiding her to sit on the edge of the bed. But I don't let her sit next to me. Instead, I take her into my arms and on top of my lap. I push her blonde locks behind her shoulders and look up into her eyes, desperate to make this right.

"Babe, listen to me," I say. "Nothing happened with Nina. After you broke things off with me, it's true that she did text me and I did tell her to come over, but only because she wanted to see Sadie. She spent the entire time she was there ignoring Sadie and talking about some new guy she's been fucking. I think she was trying to make me jealous and when that didn't work, she did try to suggest we have sex and I told her to fuck off," I say, trying to get all the information out as fast as I can.

Drew's face is twisted up with so many emotions and I don't know if she believes me or not. "Okay," she says.

"Okay?" I ask.

"Okay, I believe you," she says, wrapping her arms around my neck.

Oh thank Christ.

"Can I ask you a question?" she breathes into my neck.

"Of course," I say, running my fingers through her hair.

"Do you wish I were more...I don't know. Like her? Or like the other women who come into the shop?" she asks, pulling away from me, her eyes downcast.

"First of all, no. I definitely don't wish you were like Nina at fucking all. But what exactly do you mean by the other women?" I ask.

"You know. More tattoos, tighter clothes, more makeup," she says.

"I'm going to stop you right there," I say. "Because while I will gladly put more ink on your body if you want, whether you have it or not is not a marker for my attraction to you. You can be a beautiful woman with or without tattoos. You're most beautiful when you're in love with how you look."

"And no," I add, "I don't want you to fucking put on skintight bodysuits and wear nine pounds of makeup or do any of that. I think you're sexiest when you're wearing nothing at all," I whisper, running my hand up her thigh.

"Now," I continue, "I'm not going to stop you if you want to paint your face up. Just know, I'll probably always want to smudge your lipstick. And I'm not going to stop you if you want to wear something tight or that shows some skin. I'm not an insecure lover. I will proudly show you off. But I will most definitely protest if you put those god awful long fake fingernails on that make me have to open your Cokes for you."

This causes her to giggle and I laugh, too. "Seriously, how do you even safely wipe your own lady bits with those things on?" I ask.

She giggles again and says, "I don't know, but I've had those same exact thoughts."

Seriously, a good long nail is one thing. A ravenous raptor claw is quite another.

"Are we done with this now, babe?" I ask. "Can we make out now?"

She cradles my face with her hands, pressing her lips to mine, parting my mouth with her tongue, kissing me deeply. A low growl forms in the back of my throat as she sinks her teeth into my bottom lip.

"You are the devil," I whisper against her mouth.

"Only around you," she says.

A man can live with that.

TWO IS BETTER THAN ONE
DREW

When I come into work on Thursday, we're closed, but I'm not sure why.

"Tradition," Will says.

Everyone is gathered around and Will is holding a hat but no one is saying anything else. They pass the hat around the circle, each of them taking a slip of paper and I'm the last to go. I pull out a small slip and hand the hat back to Will.

"Drew, before you open it, there's something you should know. We have a Secret Santa party every year in the Spring as a peaceful form of rebellion," she says.

"Against what?" I ask.

Will looks around the circle. Hawk looks at Will and then to me.

"We have no idea," Hanson says.

Everyone erupts with laughter and begins opening their slips of paper. Mine says *Will* and I'm both super excited and nervous because now I have to think about what to get her.

"The party is on Sunday night," she says. "Hawk's place."

I nod, slipping the paper into the front pocket of my jeans and walking to Hawk.

"Hey there," he says.

"Hello, you," I say. I wrap my arms around him and squeeze tight.

"We're going somewhere today," he says.

"We are?" I ask.

"Yep, today is the day. Everyone is going," he says.

"Where? When?" I ask.

"As soon as Ava gets here," he says.

Where on earth could the entire gang be going?

———

AS PROMISED, AS SOON AS AVA HITS THE DOOR OF Bird's Eye, we caravan to the suburbs, dogs and all. Will keeps texting me from the other car about how if she has to hear one more *dude* between Avery and Hanson, she might throw herself from the window while still in motion and I'm laughing as we pull up to a large house on a dead-end street.

I look around and the neighborhood is so...normal. Bright green, freshly cut grass on each manicured lawn, clean white siding, pristine cars in most of the driveways. It's not a super rich neighborhood but it's upper middle class for sure.

"Where are we?" I ask.

"Home," Hawk says, hopping out of the Jeep and coming around to help me and Ava out.

I watch Will and the guys pile out of the car behind us and gather stuff from their trunk. *Is that gift wrap? What's going on?*

Just then, the door to the house we're parked in front of

opens, an older petite woman waving from it. Her heather gray hair is pulled back in a bun, a floral apron wrapped neatly around her small waist. "You're here!" she yells toward us.

I lean in and ask Will, "Who is that?"

"Hawk's mom," she says, smiling at me.

I gulp and feel my hands start to tremble. *Holy shit. His mom?! Don't panic. Don't panic. Don't panic.*

A man who looks about Hawk's age, or maybe a little older, walks out behind her and I hear Will cuss.

"Oh fuck," she says.

"What's wrong?" I ask.

"Nothing. I, uh, I just didn't know Derek was going to be here," she says, wringing her hands.

Oh. Derek. Hawk's older brother. The *other* Tanner.

I assess the man from a distance, noticing almost immediately they don't look much alike. Not that Derek is unattractive. He's definitely not. But where Hawk's hair is almost jet black, Derek's hair is a soft, medium brown. Maybe it's just that he holds his face differently, but his features are far less severe. Though I suspect with provocation, they could be just as menacing. He's just as tall, basically just as broad, but all around less...bad boy looking. I think they said he was a doctor. So his more welcoming demeanor makes sense, I guess.

"Hey, Willette," Derek says.

My eyes grow wide, as I rarely hear anyone use her full name. Hawk uses it occasionally when they're picking on each other. She hates it almost as much as her middle name. But Derek says it with such sincerity. And to my surprise, she doesn't react as I expect her to.

"Hi," Will says. Her voice sounds so different talking to him.

So soft compared to how she sounds at the shop, or even alone with me.

"You must be Drew," he says, walking straight to me and wrapping his arms around me.

Okay, they sort of have the same hug, minus the part where Hawk feels me up. "Um, yes," I say.

"My brother is a hugger," Hawk says.

Derek releases me and goes to greet his brother.

"We've heard so much about you." This comment comes to me from his mother, which shocks me to a nearly paralyzed state, and I don't know what to say in return. "And you!" She turns to Ava.

"Me?" Ava says.

"Of course. My son says you're quite the artist," she says. His mother turns back to me and smiles. "Now, let's get inside so one of these men can cook us some food." She takes me by the arm and guides me up the sidewalk.

Oh god. Don't panic.

Everyone is in the kitchen, placing gifts on the table, and I pull Hawk to the side just long enough to get two quiet moments in.

"What are we doing here?" I ask.

"It's my mom's birthday," he says.

"Oh my god. You should've told me. I didn't get her anything," I say, panicking.

"Relax. I took care of it. But I knew if I tried telling you, you would protest, and I wanted you to meet her," he says.

Well, he's right about that. I definitely would have protested and panicked, then protested some more. But I guess having Will and the other guys here softens the meet. It's like a gathering, which is a nice setting for this.

"I have to go help my brother on the grill or we'll all be eating hockey pucks," he says.

"I heard that," his brother yells from across the room.

"Are you going to be okay?" he asks.

I nod my head stiffly, because yes. I can do this. I'm capable of being a normal, sociable person.

Hawk kisses my cheek, hands me a glass of wine, and disappears to help Derek. Ava plays out in the yard with Raven and Sadie, leaving me alone with Will and Hawk's mom. Avery and Hanson stand close to the grill, laughing and joking with the Tanner brothers.

I glance over at Will, and she's not her normal bubbly self. Her words and actions are very measured.

"What's wrong?" I ask.

"Nothing," she says. "Just tired, I guess."

"Tired of harboring something like a twenty-year-old crush on my son," Momma Tanner says, and I choke, spitting my wine out.

Oh. My God.

"Shhhhh," Will whispers.

"Oh, relax," she says. "They can't hear us."

I glance over at the men, who are definitely too far away to hear us, making it impossible for Gail's shocking confession to faze them.

"Derek is the crush?" I whisper.

Will cradles her face in her hands. "Yes," she groans.

Wow. I immediately turn back and look at Derek again, wanting a more thorough assessment. I guess I understand what she meant when she said she and her crush are very different people. Doctor Derek Tanner looks like a very normal guy. If he has tattoos, I can't see them.

"Don't let him fool you," Will says. "When he rolls his sleeves up, he's covered in tattoos. Just none visible when he's working."

Oh. Okay, Doctor Derek. I see you. Good guy exterior. Bad boy core.

The brothers laugh together with ease, and it makes me happy in a strange sort of way to see Hawk so happy. I wonder again for a moment what it would have been like to have a sibling. Then I look at Will and the guys and decide it doesn't matter. Because the family I want is the family I have now.

HOUSE OF MEMORIES
HAWK

"Since when do you bring women home, little brother?" Derek asks, flipping a burger on the grill and elbowing me in the ribs.

"Since one was worth bringing home," I say.

His eyebrows shoot up because I've never brought a woman home. Much less a single mother with a kid. Women and I have always been complicated. Until Drew, I haven't exactly attracted what anyone would consider *bring home to the family* material.

"Does she know?" he asks.

"Know what?"

"That you're loaded?" he says.

I don't know why Derek says it like this. We're not exactly *loaded*, but we don't have to worry about money. I mean, I can't go out and buy a private jet or my own island or anything. I definitely wouldn't describe us as *rich* but I don't exactly blink at buying Drew all new furniture either.

"She probably has an idea that I'm okay on money," I say.

Derek narrows his eyes at me, assessing the situation in the big brotherly way he does. "So you don't think—"

"Don't even suggest it," I bite, cutting him off.

Derek raises his hands up in defeat. "Just trying to look out for you, little brother." He takes a swig of his beer.

Hanson and Avery walk closer, ending the conversation that would've definitely ended in me punching Derek. I know he's my big brother and I know he's only mentioning it to look out for me, but it's not something I'm worried about with Drew. And it's definitely not something he needs to bring up now, at our mother's house with everyone here. As a matter of fact, he can piss off with that insinuation.

I look up at the patio where Drew is sitting with my mom and Will, all of them laughing and chatting. I watch the delicate features of Drew's face light up and I'm overcome with a deep satisfaction that I decided to bring her.

My eye catches Ava running, and I turn to watch her being playfully chased by the dogs. Her arms are spread out wide and she's flapping them like a bird or maybe a fairy. I don't really know what little girls pretend to be.

She stops just shy of the picnic table and heaves to catch her breath.

"Hey, kid," I say, walking over to her for a moment and leaving the guys. "What were you doing over there?" I ask her, pointing to where she was previously flapping her arms.

"I was pretending to be a baby hawk," Ava says.

———

THE REST OF THE EVENING PLAYS OUT LIKE A DREAM. Everyone sits down together to eat on the patio, all swapping stories, but of course, my mother has the most. She pulls out ancient tales of much younger Tanner brothers and we spend most of the evening defending our younger selves' actions to our friends. It's okay, though. It's my mother's favorite part of gatherings. And who would we be to deny her such happiness on her birthday?

Sometimes I wish she wasn't alone, that she'd found someone through the years who became her companion. If you ask her, she'll tell you she prefers it this way, that she has all the love she needs in her sons and friends. But I think she just doesn't want to admit it.

At the end of the night, we gather at the front door to say our goodbyes and I watch Derek pull Drew into a hug, whispering to her. Their conversation looks to be more than a cursory exchange and I worry about what my brother might say to her considering his remarks to me earlier at the grill.

"She's a good one, I think," my mom says, holding her arms out to hug my neck.

I lean down, giving into her, returning her embrace. "I think so too," I say.

"Take care of each other," she whispers, kissing my cheek.

"I'll do my best, Momma. Happy birthday," I say.

She releases me from her embrace and pats my cheek, turning to say her goodbyes to Will.

After what seems like a full hour of saying goodbye, we're back in the Jeep on our way home. Ava's passed out in the back, the dogs curled up with her. Drew has my hand in her lap, drawing circles on the back with her thumb. Despite the difference in size, our hands fit together perfectly, her small fingers laced between my large ones.

My thoughts flip through the evening, replaying all the moments I made eye contact with Drew across the table. Each time, her eyes were illuminated and warm. She seemed so happy.

"What did my brother say to you when we left?" I ask her, breaking the silence.

Drew's head snaps to look at me, seemingly startled that I've interrupted the peaceful drive back with my question. "Um, you know, he was just being a good big brother," she says.

My grip tightens on the steering wheel. "What does that mean?" I ask.

She lets out a long sigh, hesitant to go on. "He just...he wanted to make sure I was with you for the right reasons. That I actually cared."

"He shouldn't have said that to you," I say, my voice more rigid than I want it to be.

"Sure he should've. He's just looking out for you. Hawk, you're a catch. You own your own business. You inherited money when your father died. I mean, I can see it. Women could want to be with you for the wrong reasons. For free tattoos or your money. I know those women. I hope I've shown you I'm not one of them, but I can still see his concern. I have a child. I'm a single mom. He's just being a brother to you. I didn't take it personally."

I really don't like anything she's saying. I don't like that he talked to her about this, that he brought any of this up to her.

It's true in the past I've weeded out some women early for telling behavior. After a few dates, they'll ask me to tattoo them and expect it to be free. Or if we make it past that, they find out about the money I've inherited and suddenly there are just all these things they want to buy and hint at me.

As the years went on, I picked up on it faster and faster. Probably why I never brought anyone home. Probably why I found myself in a relationship with Nina, who had her own money. But, have I tattooed her for free? Yes. Did I pay her to get my dog back? Also yes. So, even when I think it's okay, clearly it's not. Probably why I grew more and more cold toward people in general honestly. Or at least most of them.

"I guess he's been witness to some things in my past. But still, I'm sorry," I finally say.

"And I'm sorry those things happened to you. That those women didn't appreciate you. Although...I'm not too sorry. Because, well, now you're mine." She grins, leaning over the center console and pressing a kiss to my cheek.

"And I'm sorry about the things that have happened to you. But not too sorry..."

Drew smiles when I trail off, kissing me again. It seems we both realize what we've been through has put us where we are and we're okay with that.

"Now, wanna try out that new bed?" she asks.

I turn to see her wiggling her eyebrows at me, her smile stretching into something a little more devilish.

And I would love nothing more than to try out that new fucking bed.

NICEST THING
DREW

To my relief, the rebellious Secret Santa in Spring gift exchange was delayed to a full two weeks later. Can I just say what a glorious two weeks they have been? Most evenings were spent with Hawk either at his place or mine. Weekends were reserved for trips to local places he thought Ava and I might like. Last weekend, he took us to an interactive art museum. Some rooms were look-only, while others let you become part of the art. Some even let you create your own. Needless to say, Ava had a blast. Each night spent with him has been a hurricane of sweet moments and sexy naughty times. It's enough to make my head spin.

Ava and I arrive at Hawk's apartment, my gift for Will in hand. We're greeted by literally everyone as it seems we're the last to arrive, and Ava blames it on my makeup routine.

Hawk crosses from the living room to embrace me, immediately wrapping his arms around me and kissing my lips. "I know it's only been like two hours since I saw you at work, but I missed you," he whispers.

Will makes an audible gagging noise from behind him. "Okay, love birds, let's just pack that away for later and get to the part where we all get gifts, huh?" she says.

Everyone gathers in the living room, a pile of presents on the coffee table much larger than should be for just five people exchanging. *Were we supposed to get several gifts?* As panic starts to rise in my chest, Hanson speaks.

"Here you go, *princesa*," he says, handing Ava a gift.

"For me?" she says.

"But of course," Hanson says, looking around. "You think we'd all exchange gifts and not get our Ava something?"

Tears swell in my eyes. *Our Ava*, he said. Before we came tonight, I made it clear to Ava not to expect gifts because this was a grownup thing. But as I watch Avery give her a gift next, and then Will, I'm overcome with emotion. While each of us are only exchanging one gift, they've all taken the time to get Ava something in addition.

I blink the salt water away, rubbing at the corners with my index fingers.

"You okay?" Hawk whispers to me.

I nod, unable to form words.

He kisses my temple and smiles. To Ava, he says, "Here's one from me, too."

Like he hasn't given her enough. Like her whole room couldn't have counted for this.

She thanks them all as she starts to rip paper from the first.

"Okay, now us!" Will says, her enthusiasm so endearing. She's practically giddy.

"Here you go, dude," Hanson says, handing Hawk a package.

Hawk opens the small box, a bottle of what appears to be a very Irish, very expensive whiskey inside.

Everyone starts to give their gifts to one another after that, and I hand mine to Will, excited to see her reaction.

She runs her hands over the somewhat flat package before ripping the paper down the front. She gasps as soon as she realizes what it is. "Oh my god, how did you get this?" she yells.

"It took me a few days, but I can't say exactly. You might die," I answer.

She looks down in her hand at the vinyl record of her favorite band, *The Honorary Title*. Their 2004 album *Anything but the Truth* being her absolute favorite, I managed to acquire a vinyl copy, the signatures of each band member scribbled in Sharpie on the outside. Inside the package is some other band merchandise, including a T-shirt and stickers. I guess this wouldn't be as big of a deal, but the band broke up a few years ago. Apparently, that was a very dark time for her.

"No really, how did you even find this?" she asks.

"I may have stalked some band members on Instagram," I admit.

Will's eyes grow wide, her face serious. "That works?" she says, pulling out her phone.

I laugh, because of course Will would pull out her phone to see if she can stalk them until they talk to her. I'm mostly relieved she likes it because I spent the first two days after drawing her name completely freaking out about what to get her. I thought back to all the conversations we had about what she likes, what she reads, what she listens to. I recalled a very specific conversation we had about this band having a reunion show at some point, and how it broke Will's heart not to be able to go. So this band seemed like the right place to start for a gift idea.

"Your turn," Hawk says, placing a package in my hand. It's large and flat.

"You pulled my name?" I asked, squinting my eyes at him.

"I may have traded for it," he admits. "But, I also got you two things." Hawk places another small box on top of the large flat one.

It...looks like a jewelry box. The panic in my chest returns because what the hell? More jewelry? And this looks like a ring box. *Surely he didn't get me a ring.*

I place the small box on the couch next to me and start with the big one, ripping the paper right down the front. And then I can't breathe. Inside is a painting, of mine and Ava's faces smiling. Frozen in brush strokes. My fingertips find my trembling bottom lip.

"Do you like it?" he asks, voice low and serious. "I thought I could hang it above your couch if you want."

"I love it. It's the best gift I've ever received," I say, holding back sniffles.

Hawk watches me as my eyes move over the canvas again and again. He's so talented. And now I understand what he meant when he was talking about everyone in the shop being great artists off skin, too.

"And now this one. Although, it probably won't top that one," he says. He places the small box in my hand, a simple red bow wrapped around a black box.

I hesitate, my heart pounding so hard in my chest, I think it might break right out of my ribcage. I finger the bow, pulling at the ribbon so slowly, time might actually be standing still.

Pulling the top from the box, a glint of silver reflects up from inside, and my breath catches. *I'm freaking out. What is happening? Oh. My. God.*

It's a...key? I pick it up, holding it between my thumb and index finger, staring at it in confusion.

"It's to here, my place," he whispers.

"A key to your loft?" I clarify.

Hawk nods, almost sheepishly.

"So like, I could come over at two in the morning and raid your fridge if I'm out of snacks?" I tease.

"It appears so," he says, laughing.

I lean in closer to him, making sure the rest of the group can't hear us. "Or like, I could come over at three in the morning and crawl under the blankets between your legs and do that thing you like with my tongue?"

"I would definitely love it if you did that," he says, in that growl of his.

I giggle and bite his ear, knowing exactly the type of response this will get me.

"I have something else planned. Something not in the gift pile but already arranged," he says.

"What's that?" I ask.

"Tomorrow after work, we're taking a weekend trip. Just you and me. Will can watch Ava if that's okay with you?" he says.

"I suppose I don't get to ask where we're going?"

"Do you ever?" He laughs.

This man and his surprises. Not that I'm complaining. I don't think I'll ever grow tired of them.

CRASH INTO ME
HAWK

To be clear, I didn't want to give Drew a key to my place. I wanted to ask her to move in with me. But that felt crazy after only dating for a short time. Then again, I can be a little crazy. And impulsive. Which is why I sought Will's advice on it. Which is when she told me I was fucking crazy and impulsive. The key to my place was the compromise.

"Are you in love with her?" she'd asked me.

"What's that got to do with it?" I asked back.

"You don't go moving people into your place if you're not in love," she told me.

I didn't really have any room to argue with her because I moved Nina in without loving her and look how that turned out. But then I started asking myself whether or not I was in love with Drew. And that was a pretty good fucking question to ask myself because I'm pretty sure I've only been in love once and that was with Becky Shemansky in the tenth grade. She had curly brown hair and braces that cut my lip every time we made out.

But I kept making out with her because she let me touch her boobies. And I was a teenage boy, so that earned me a lot of locker room points or whatever the fuck I was concerned with at the time.

So, all week I've been asking myself: *Do I love her? Am I in love with her?* And the answer is always the same. *That's a good fucking question.* Which is sort of a non-answer. And I've resigned to thinking if I can't answer it yet, then maybe I'm not quite in love with her just yet. I mean, I love spending time with her —and Ava.

I love being around Drew. I love the sex. I love who she is as a person, who she is as a mother, as a lover. So maybe being *in* love is just right around the corner. A natural progression.

These thoughts are still swirling in my mind as I drop Will and the dogs off at Drew's apartment and pick Drew up for our weekend away. We're finally in the Jeep on our way out of town, my hand in hers on the center console, and this has become one of my favorite things. I don't think I can accurately describe the comfort and peace that washes over me when her hand is in mine and she's drawing circles on the back of it. Sometimes she looks down and traces the tattoos on my skin, over my knuckles and up my forearm, causing goosebumps to ripple all the way down my spine.

"What are you thinking about?" she asks, cutting into my thoughts.

"You," I say simply.

"What about me?" Drew leans closer to me, over the console, and props her chin on her hand, letting mine go.

I let out a long sigh. "I'm thinking about how much of the weekend I can keep you naked," I say. A little white lie. Okay, well not totally a white lie, because it's definitely crossed my mind a few times. But, I also can't tell her I'm wondering if I love her or not. That would just be weird.

"A lot, I hope." She grins.

God I love it when she does that. "And I'm hoping you like where I'm taking you."

"I'm sure I will. I could have fun with you anywhere," she says. Drew leans her head against my shoulder and turns the music up.

We spend the rest of the drive in a comfortable silence, my thoughts volleying between questioning love like some kind of philosopher and sexy fun time like a horny man child. What a crazy train.

———

WE WIND DOWN THE LONG GRAVEL DRIVEWAY UNTIL we find ourselves parked in front of Maple Ridge Bed & Breakfast. I spoke to the owners on the phone and they told me they had no other guests this weekend, so the place is all ours. Which means I won't feel quite as bad when I make Drew do that little squeal she does when I double tap my fingers in that one place she likes.

"A bed and breakfast?" she asks, her eyes running over the large Victorian house in front of us and the well-manicured property surrounding it.

"You like it?" I ask.

"I love it! I've never been to one," she says.

I grab our bags from the back and check in, then we meet Carl and Nancy, the owners. They're a lovely gray-haired couple that tells us they have seventeen grandchildren and that breakfast will be served in the dining hall at eight. Then, they hand me the keys to the Oak Suite, the largest room they offer.

"Your private dinner will be served on the terrace at six, as requested," Nancy says, showing us up the stairs.

Our room is exactly what you'd expect in a bed and breakfast run by an elderly couple. The Oak Suite is named such because all the furniture inside is, in fact, oak. A king bed sits in the center with a lace canopy over top. A small balcony to the left overlooks the gardens and the rest of the room is pretty basic. All oak furniture and a wingback chair.

"Oh, look at this," Drew says, standing at the entrance of the private bathroom.

I walk over and peer inside, lifting an eyebrow at the jacuzzi tub that sits next to the glass-encased shower. "Oh, I like that," I say. "Yes indeed."

"Should we...shower before dinner?" she asks, leaning her face in close to my neck, nibbling my skin.

I reach back and pull my shirt up over my head with one hand. "That's a brilliant idea."

We can't get into the bathroom or shower fast enough, both of us removing clothes, kicking off shoes, and pulling at each other in a frenzy. I stop touching her long enough to turn on the water, while she throws her hair up in a messy bun on top of her head.

Within seconds, the whole bathroom is full of steam, the shower glass fogged over, and I press her into it. My mouth travels from hers, down her sternum and over her tits. I hitch her leg up, pinning her to the glass with my body, sliding between her thighs.

"We didn't bring a condom in here," she rasps through labored breaths.

"Are you on birth control?"

"Yes," she says.

"Oh god, tell me I can, Drew. Please," I beg, rubbing myself against her entrance.

"Please, yes," she whispers between whimpers.

I push inside her, succumbing to her request, to my own desires. She takes me by the mouth, lapping her tongue against mine. If I didn't know any better, I'd swear we were literally trying to devour each other. And maybe, to a certain extent, we are.

I take her in the shower, no barrier between us, all the thoughts from this week gone. She feels so fucking good wrapped around me, wet and warm. But more than that, she makes me feel alive.

In love or not, Drew is all I want.

THE CHEMICALS BETWEEN US
DREW

Please be advised, no one got clean in that shower. In fact, that's the dirtiest shower I've ever taken. I need a shower just to wash away the delicious filth of it all.

While Hawk is in the bathroom getting ready, I slip into one of the dresses I brought with me because I was told we *might do some nice things*. That's about all the instruction I got for packing.

I'm putting the finishing touches on my makeup in front of the dresser mirror when Hawk finally exits the bathroom. *And he's wearing a suit*. Let me correct that statement, as my eyes sweep over him starting at his black dress shoes, working up his tight black dress pants, trailing over the pressed white button-up. Because it's not buttoned all the way and he's without a tie, choosing to let the tattoos of his chest and neck peek out. My eyes continue over the lapels of his matching black suit jacket and come to rest on his face because goddamn he has a beautiful face. All the vagina butterflies have been released and they're fluttering about and I feel like I can't breathe.

A low whistle escapes his lips. "Aren't you a vision," he says, his eyes trailing up my bare thighs.

Admittedly, this dress is short. Very short. As in *I better not need to bend over* short. "This old thing?" I tease.

Hawk walks to me, leans down and runs his hand up my bare thigh, his hand disappearing beneath the edge of the thin material.

"Don't do that. We'll never make it to dinner," I whisper. I'm breathless under his touch.

He presses a kiss to my lips, reluctantly removing his hand from the warmth of my skin, pouting all the while. "Fine. But I already know what I'm having for dessert," he hints, taking my hand in his and pressing a kiss to the back of it, grazing his teeth slowly over my knuckles.

A trail of goosebumps spreads over the back of my neck and in a momentary state of euphoria, I almost agree to skip dinner.

"Come on," I say, leading him from the room before neither of us leave it for the entire weekend.

I will say one thing, though. Dinner was delicious. As was breakfast the next morning. As was the after-breakfast morning sex we had before we left to explore some local tourist shops.

I told Hawk I wanted to get Ava a souvenir or two and maybe one for Will as a thank you for babysitting. So while we explore, we're also on the hunt.

"Oh, let's go in here," I say, pointing to a boho-looking shop with jewelry and trinkets in the window.

"Okay, but after this, I want lunch and I definitely want ice cream," Hawk says.

I flip through T-shirts while Hawk looks through the jewelry on a nearby shelf. I hold up a T-shirt with a bouquet of flowers on it, a dagger in the middle of them. "I think I found a shirt for Will," I say, laughing.

"And I think I found something for Ava," Hawk says, walking over to me and holding out his hand. A small silver chain dangles from his fingers with a bird charm attached. "We're all part of the Bird's Eye family. Even her," he says.

I smile and nod my approval to him, knowing she'll love it.

After buying the items, we cross the street to a small restaurant with a patio for lunch.

"I got you something too," he says.

"What, while I was distracted at the register?" I laugh.

"Precisely," he says, pulling out a petite silver chain and handing it to me. It's larger than the one he showed me for Ava but has the same bird charm hanging from it.

"Now you can match," he says. "My little birds."

I put the chain around my neck, pressing it to my chest, and smile at him. For whatever reason, this necklace, though a fraction of the cost, feels more significant than the diamond he gave me.

"Thank you. I love it," I say.

After we're seated at the restaurant, Hawk reaches across the table and takes my hand, lacing our fingers together. To anyone else, we might look lovesick. *Love. Whoa. Did I just think that? Just slow down, missy.* I'm sure Hawk hasn't been thinking about the L-bomb. I push those thoughts deep down into the pits of some far-off place and focus.

It's obviously way too soon to be thinking about love. *Isn't it?* I try to think back to when Curtis and I were still just dating. *How long was it before I loved him?* For whatever reason, my mind can't do the math. It's extremely difficult for me to put *love* and

Curtis in the same train of thought at all anymore, past or present.

Hawk and I have a delicious lunch, chatting about several different topics, my thoughts about love mostly at bay. Then, we make our way through a few more shops. He finds the most atrocious tarantula paperweight as a gift for Avery. It's like a real tarantula—or *was*, once. Maybe it was a taxidermy project. But the big hairy thing is cast in resin in an octagon shape. The whole thing makes me laugh but also sort of creeps me out. We find a tacky miniature lion sculpture for Hanson. Apparently getting each other terrible gifts is a thing they do all the time.

When we get back to our room at the bed and breakfast, I try feeling Hawk up as soon as we set our shopping bags down.

"Not yet." He smiles.

"No?" I pout.

"We're going for a walk before dinner. After that we'll have sexy time in the Jacuzzi tub," he says, smirking.

I have to agree, as I like his overall envisioned plan for the evening. "Okay, let's go."

"Why the rush?" he teases, his large hands gripping my hips.

"Not rushing, just eagerly trying to get the fun started," I say, leaning up to wrap my arms around his neck. I press my lips to his, biting into the bottom one the way I know he likes, hearing his sharp intake of breath.

"Okay, yeah. Let's go before I lose my mind and skip to the end," he says, ushering me out the door.

WHAT IS LOVE?
HAWK

This is it. A culmination of the day's events. The shops were fun, and lunch was great. Walking the trails all over the property were beautiful. Dinner was delicious. But this is what I've been looking forward to all day. And I've been a good boy. So excuse me while I stand here and watch as Drew slowly undresses, before lowering herself into the jacuzzi. The bubbles from the jets create just enough static on top of the water to obscure my vision of her flesh, and my own thoughts are teasing me.

I step into the hot water, steam rising, feeling all the rigidity in my muscles melt away. I make a mental note to check on the cost of having one of these installed in the loft because holy shit, this is amazing.

"Wow," Drew says, her single word coming out more like a moan. "This should be illegal."

"I think I should have one of these installed in my place." I lean my head back on the little headrest and shut my eyes.

"One more reason for me to use that key," she says.

We sit in silence for a few long minutes, soaking in the relaxation of the jets, the soothing hot water melting away our stress. I hear the water move between us, feel her hands on my knees.

"You're too far away," she whispers.

"You're right," I reply.

Drew straddles me, pressing her naked torso to mine. I wrap my hands around her, cupping her ass to hold her in place. She runs her wet hands through my hair and I feel tiny droplets of water run down my neck, sending a shiver right through me.

My fingers trail up her spine until they reach her hair and tug, exposing her throat to me. I kiss the delicate muscles there as she swallows. Her fingers dig into the flesh of my shoulders and her back arches, her body pushing into mine.

"I want you," she says, lowering her mouth to my ear. I grip her tighter, my fingers digging into the soft meat of her hips.

"Do you want to get out first?" I ask.

She's moaning against my neck, licking and sucking and biting. "I want you like this, in here," she urges.

"Are you sure?" I press my hips against hers, teasing.

She nods, blowing hot breath against my skin. "Please," she says, her tone begging.

And that's pretty much all it takes for me to topple like a house of cards. She glides against me and I realign her, pushing myself inside her. She bends and twists with pleasure, releasing moans into the quiet bathroom, the small space lending an acoustic value, sending an echo bouncing from wall to wall.

"Do you like the way I make you feel?" I groan against her neck.

"Yes," she whispers, between short, ragged breaths.

"Do you want more?" I ask.

"Yes," she says.

It drives me wild to ask her things, hear her answers, to know how she's feeling, to watch her face twist in pleasure. It drives me wild to know I'm responsible for making her feel the way she does. Any man worth his salt in bed is concerned with how the woman feels. Don't let anyone tell you any differently.

I push into her, over and over, until I feel her body shudder and collapse on top of me. Then I go. Because ladies first, in all things.

We crawl into bed later, still naked but hey, at least we're dry. She curls into me and I wrap myself around her as completely as I can, throwing a leg over hers, cradling her head on my bicep with my other arm wrapped around her. I gently stroke her hair, tucking it behind her ear as we talk about the weekend, about how we both wish it wasn't coming to an end tomorrow, and we make plans to have more weekends like this in the future.

I'm overcome with emotions I barely understand. Planning future weekends feels so right, yet so foreign. I've never done this with anyone. Then again, I've never done any of this with anyone. Not like this.

I feel Drew's breathing slow, her body relaxing into mine. Her voice sounds sleepier now as she says, "Thank you for this weekend."

"Of course," I whisper against her ear.

"I'm having such a good time," she says, and I know it won't be long before she's asleep.

This is how it is most nights I'm with her. She falls asleep before I do. Sometimes I watch her for a little while, listening to her breathing. She feels so at peace, looks so at peace, I can't help myself.

"I'm glad you like it," I whisper back.

And I can't explain it. I don't know exactly when I decided or how or what drives me to the urge. But I lean in close, my lips hovering just above the skin of her cheek.

"Hey, Drew?" I whisper.

"Yeah?"

"I love you."

Drew is silent, only the steady rhythm of her breathing filling the air. Her body shrugs up and down as she inhales and exhales. She's asleep. I thought I was going to say it in time. But it's a swing and a miss.

I just told her I love her and she's not even conscious.

UNACCOMMODATING
DREW

P anic. Throat constricting. Full on mini stroke. Brain shutting down. More panic.

Yes, I pretended to be sleeping last night when Hawk told me he loved me, okay? I did. I couldn't help it. I panicked.

I floated out of my body, and apparition Drew watched herself lying next to Hawk while he whispered he loved her into her ear and she almost kept floating straight up to the pearly gates. *I'm a coward, okay? A big, fat coward.*

I didn't know what else to do. I heard the words leave his mouth. I did. But my throat closed up the instant I heard him say it. *I don't know why. I don't. Maybe I do. Okay, now I'm rambling to myself.*

We woke up this morning, still wrapped up in each other. Had slow, passionate sex with lots of petting and eye contact. I realized only after, when we got up from the bed and began to dress, that we weren't just having sex. We were making love. We were full on loving the shit out of each other with our bodies.

So then I panicked again and *used the bathroom* for like twelve minutes. By the time I came out, Hawk had already gotten fully dressed and packed both our bags.

Of course, he's been really quiet this morning. Perhaps because he's trying to figure out a way to tell me again while I'm for sure awake THAT HE LOVES ME. *More panic.*

"Are we ready to go?" I ask, slipping on my shoes as I scan the room for any miscellaneous items we may have forgotten.

"I think so," he says, rubbing the back of his neck with the palm of his hand.

I know he does this when he's thinking, when he's bothered by something. And I'm sure, given last night and this morning, he's probably quite bothered.

"Can we grab some coffee on the way? I could really use some iced caramel deliciousness in my life," I say, trying to keep the conversation light.

"Wait, before we go, there's something I need to say," he says, cupping his hand around my shoulder and turning me to face him. His jaw is set, eyebrows pressed together. He looks positively pained. In agony.

"What is it?" I swallow. *Oh my god. This is it.* I don't know if I'm ready to hear this for the second time, but I guess we're about to find out. I reach up and brush my hand across his cheek, wishing more than anything I could at least take away this look marring the beautiful features of his face. I watch as the muscles in his throat work up and down, the tattoos there flexing and relaxing.

"I, uh, I…" he starts, but then he pauses, letting out a long, defeated breath. "I just really hope you had a good time." Hawk puts forth his best effort to summon a smile to his lips but it feels stunted, and I don't press the issue.

"I had the absolute best time," I say. It's all I can manage.

On the ride back, it's quiet and I feel like I've betrayed him somehow. I sit the same way I always do, his hand in my lap as I draw circles on the back of it. But neither of us are really present. It feels like we're both inside our heads a hundred miles away from here and each other and it absolutely fucking sucks.

Part of me wants to tell him I know, that I heard him. But pretending not to hear him was sort of a dick thing for me to do and I don't want him to be mad at me after our wonderful weekend. Then I circle back to thinking the longer I wait, the worse it's going to feel when or if he ever discovers that truth.

We make almost the entire trip back home in complete silence, neither of us acknowledging that either. But when we get inside my apartment, it's easier to forget the awkwardness for a bit, in favor of our welcoming home.

"You're back!" Ava exclaims.

She runs to the door as we open it and bypasses me in favor of hugging Hawk first. *What a little traitor.*

"Hey, kid," he says, fluffing her hair and smiling his big, genuine toothy grin.

"How was your trip?" Will asks as we make it into the living room and sit down.

"So nice," I say, leaning back into the soft couch and sighing.

Hawk leans down to greet Raven and Sadie and we talk about the shops we visited, the food we ate, and the charm of the bed and breakfast itself. Then, we give Will her shirt and Ava her necklace.

"Now you're a bird, too," Hawk says, handing Ava the dainty chain.

I watch Ava's eyes light up and she immediately wants help

putting it on. No sooner than I clasp it for her, she is beaming, looking ten times happier and more confident in an instant.

Ava skips off to her room after a little while and Will eventually says her goodbyes, leaving me and Hawk alone again. It doesn't take long for the uncomfortable silence to settle in around us. In an effort to prevent it from happening again, I offer wine. *Because booze always helps, right?*

"Do you want to stay tonight?" I ask.

"Yeah, sure," he says. "The dogs are already here so it certainly makes it easier."

I check the clock and notice it's already time to start planning for some sort of dinner. Pulling open the fridge, I scan the contents and bite my lip at the lack of options.

"Let's just order pizza," Hawk suggests.

"Now you're talking," I say, shutting the fridge door and joining him back on the couch, where he pulls out his phone and clicks some buttons. Thanks to modern technology, you don't even have to talk to anyone to order food anymore.

I take a few sips of my wine and lean back into the fold of Hawk's arm. "I vote we just abandon all worldly responsibilities in favor of this." I sigh.

His lips graze the top of my head and I can even feel him grin. "I'm definitely in favor of that," he says.

Before I know it, I'm drifting in and out of consciousness and then I'm asleep. I suppose a nap before dinner is always a good plan.

———

THE SOUND OF A KNOCK ON MY DOOR STARTLES ME awake and I jump up from Hawk's arm, who apparently had also dozed off.

"Shit, we fell asleep. I guess this is old age," he jokes.

"That must be the pizza," I say, standing and running my hands over my clothes. "I'll grab it. You get the plates."

Hawk walks toward the kitchen as I step into the hallway leading to the front door. I swing it open, fully expecting to be greeted by some teenage delivery kid.

Instead, my nearly forgotten past has quite literally come knocking.

"Curtis?" I say, as all the color drains from my face.

BLOOD IN THE CUT
DREW

J ust like this morning at the bed and breakfast, I am in full-on panic mode. But unlike this morning, I can't seem to shut up this time around.

"What are you doing here? How did you find me? What the hell? What are you doing here?" I ask, starting to repeat myself.

Curtis puts up his hands, hushing me. "Calm down, for Christ's sake. What, I can't come see my family?" he asks.

Family? What the fuck? The nonchalance in his tone throws me off guard.

Curtis walks into the hallway, passing me, almost making it to the living room before I turn and block him.

"What are you doing here?" I demand.

"I came to see how you are, how Ava is." He nudges me out of his way, skirting around me to get to the living room. "I see you're doing okay for yourself," he scoffs, surveying the room, the new furniture.

If he only knew. As if on cue, Hawk appears from the kitchen, no doubt confused to hear a man's voice in the apartment. He stares at Curtis and Curtis stares back. A full minute passes and I feel like I can't even form a single focused thought let alone a word or sentence.

"It would appear I've interrupted something here," Curtis says, cutting through the silence first. "I'm Curtis," he says to Hawk, stepping forward a few paces. The space between the two men shrinks as Curtis sticks his hand out. "I'm Drew's husband."

"Ex-husband," I correct, interjecting behind him.

Hawk's eyes narrow at Curtis, who immediately takes a half-step back, hand still extended. But to my surprise, Hawk shakes it, though he appears as to grip it much harder than necessary. "I wish I could say it was nice to meet you," Hawk says.

"Hawk," I urge, not wanting to make the situation any worse than it already is.

He shoots me a look, clearly unconcerned with manners at this particular juncture.

"Yes, well, it took me forever to convince that aunt of yours to give me the address to the apartment," Curtis says, turning to focus his attention on me as he gives Hawk his back. "But after I left messages with her to have you call me and you didn't...well, desperate times and all that."

"Desperate times?" I repeat, as I look back down the hallway to the bedrooms.

Ava's probably lost herself in whatever she's drawing, and I hope it stays that way a little longer.

"Yes, but perhaps we shouldn't talk about this in front of your little friend here," Curtis hints, waving his hand toward Hawk.

I blink several times and pray his waving hand isn't snatched from the air by Hawk and broken like a twig. Because it's much too close to Hawk and I've never seen Hawk's face this stone cold. You could cut glass with his jaw right now. He looks nearly rabid.

"What does that mean?" I ask, crossing my arms over my chest.

"This conversation should be private, is what it means," he says, his eyes scanning my face.

I sigh as loudly as I can. Because I don't like this. I don't like how he's shown up unannounced, how he's being so casual, the way he's calling me his *wife*, us his family. And I don't like that he thinks he's back in control of the situation, trying to dictate how it should go. But it seems like the only way I'll get out of this is by hearing him out, by letting him say what he's come all this way to say. And by the looks of it, he isn't willing to divulge any of it in front of Hawk.

While part of me feels like having Hawk stick around just out of spite, I know it won't help anything.

Just then, I hear the bedroom door open, followed by small hesitant footprints on the hardwood floor.

Ava enters the living room, her face twisted with confusion, like she's looking at a ghost. "Dad?" she says, her voice shaky.

"Of course it's me, princess," Curtis says, putting his arms out for a hug.

But Ava doesn't run to him. She doesn't even walk to him. She slowly walks around him, staring at him wildly, like he's grown a second head since the last time she saw him. Instead, her hand finds Hawk's, and she shields most of her body behind him.

"It's okay, kid," Hawk whispers down to her.

"Oh, princess," Curtis says. "It's me. Don't be scared."

"What are you doing here?" Ava questions.

"I'm just here to have a little chat with your mom. As soon as your friend leaves," he says, eyeing Hawk.

Hawk's jaw flexes, clearly unhappy with the assumption that Curtis might somehow get him to leave. Which is why I hate what I'm about to say.

"Hawk, why don't you just let me find out what he wants?" I say, already exasperated with the situation.

Curtis has only been here five minutes and I'm already tired of the bullshit. On the other hand, I should consider this growth. There was a time I put up with just about anything from this man. And now? Not so much.

Hawk cranes his neck, looking at me like I've lost my mind. And maybe I have. I don't want him to go, but I feel like it's the only way to get to the bottom of this.

Hawk's free hand balls into a fist at his side and he nods. "Okay. Text me later," he says, reluctantly letting go of Ava's hand before walking past me and out the door. The dogs trail behind him, foregoing our usual goodbye routine.

"Ava, can you go play, please?" I ask her. Then, I whirl around to Curtis again, pressing my hands to my hips.

"But I'm hungry," she says.

"I'll bring you some pizza when it gets here," I tell her.

Ava skips off without another word and I'm momentarily shocked by her coldness toward her father. In many ways, I half-expected her to be excited and have little memory of what's occurred, or at least no knowledge of the big picture.

"See you later, sweetheart," Curtis says.

I roll my eyes hard. He looks at me—all smiles, completely

and totally unapologetic. *Wow*. Honestly, I don't know how one man could have this much nerve.

"Please, come sit," he says.

His invitation strikes me as a bit condescending, considering it's my couch and my apartment. He plops himself on the couch near the center, practically cutting it in half, so I have no choice but to sit closer to him than I want. Our knees practically touch, but my back is pressed as far into the arm of the couch as I can manage. Any further and I'd be pushing myself backward over this thing and plummeting to the ground. Which honestly isn't a terrible idea. But I digress.

"I'm sorry to just show up like this. I tried to call but realized you changed your number, and your aunt wouldn't give me the address. She's the only contact I have," he starts.

"What do you want?" I ask again, for what feels like the hundredth time.

"You know, I'm not that sorry though because who even is this Hawk guy and why is he hanging around? He looks like bad news. So, I'm glad I unintentionally interrupted," he goes on, avoiding my question.

"Quite frankly, it's none of your business who he is or what he was doing here. I don't owe you an explanation for anything. Now, what do you want, Curtis?" I demand, my voice firm.

"Well, I think it's my business to know who's around Ava?" he suggests.

I huff out a condescending laugh. "You weren't too worried about that when you kicked us out when we had nowhere else to go and somehow weaseled your way out of paying hardly anything and declining visitation of any kind with her." I try hard to keep my voice low. The last thing I need is Ava overhearing any of this.

Curtis recoils, but only a fraction as he straightens his shoulders and clears his throat. "Listen, I made a mistake, okay? I see that now," he says, facial features as soft as putty. I've known Curtis a long time and if I had to guess, I'd say he almost looks remorseful. Somber.

"A *mistake?*" I repeat.

"I never should've done what I did. I want you and Ava to come home where you belong." He reaches his hand forward and places it on top of mine. A small, sincere-looking smile barely makes it to his mouth, let alone his eyes.

And just like that, the world I worked so hard to rebuild is turned right back upside down by the same man who fucked it up the first time.

LOSING YOU
HAWK

Drew didn't text me last night. She also didn't come to work this morning and instead of giving me the courtesy of that text, she handled the whole thing directly with Will.

So naturally, my mind has been reeling all day. I haven't been able to concentrate on anything outside of the one appointment I had today. No additional sketches or business conducted; no decisions made to push the expansion forward. It's almost time to open up the wall finally, and I'm supposed to make decisions with the renovation team about when to tear down said wall, when the shop will close, and ultimately, when to have a grand reopening as the newly expanded Bird's Eye. Unfortunately, my mind is so far gone today, there's no way I can focus on a calendar or counting days. Hell, I'm not even sure I put on matching socks this morning.

I tried sending Drew a couple of texts, but in an effort not to appear completely pathetic, my limit was two. After she left the second one unanswered, I had to shove my phone in my pocket and ignore it.

So imagine my surprise when I open the door to my place and Drew's perched on my couch, a dog under each hand, patiently waiting for me.

I quickly cross the floor and she stands, but makes no attempt to embrace me, which stops me in my tracks a few paces short of her.

"Hi," she says, her voice barely a whisper.

"Hey." I wait for something more, but I'm not sure what. Anything to break the silence, to reassure me or comfort me. When nothing comes, I say, "Are you okay?"

She nods. "I just needed a minute to think."

Well, shit. That can't be good. That's never good. "About what? And where's Ava?"

"With Curtis," she says.

My shoulders stiffen at her response and it takes some serious effort not to react negatively. The mere idea of him being in charge of her or caring for her makes me feel a certain way. Sure, he's her father. I'm sure he's fine and perfectly capable. But after what he did, I don't think he deserves the privilege or trust.

"What's going on, Drew?" I ask.

"Curtis said he came to tell me he made a mistake and that he wants me and Ava to come back home," she says, pushing the words out in one breath as quickly as she can.

I let a noise out that falls somewhere between a laugh and a huff. "You can't be serious?"

"Serious about what?" she asks.

"Please don't tell me you actually believe him? That he's sincere? That's he changed?" I say, my voice growing louder.

She steps back a fraction, the back of her legs hitting the couch. "I don't know what to think. People can be sorry, can't they?"

"Of course people can be sorry. People can do awful, terrible things to you and one day they can circle back and tell you they're sorry. The kicker is maybe they even mean it. But it doesn't mean you owe them your forgiveness. It doesn't mean you have to let them back in," I say, exhaling afterward. I run my fingers through my hair, unable to believe what I'm hearing.

"I'm not letting him back in," she says.

My eyes grow wide. "No?"

"At least not for me. But don't you think Ava deserves to have her dad? To know him? If she wants to?" she asks.

"Fathers and dads are two very different things, Drew," I say. I can't even stop myself; I have to laugh.

She bites her bottom lip, shifting from one foot to the other, but says nothing.

"Let me see if I get this straight. I really want to make sure I have this right," I say. "You have an absolute panic attack over me, thinking I might, *maybe*, one day abandon you and Ava the way your fuckface ex-husband did, so you break things off with me. But, the actual fuckface ex-husband who's done this before gets to just walk right back in?" I shake my head, unable to see the logic in the situation. And maybe I shouldn't have called him a fuckface, but it felt good and I won't apologize for it.

"That's not what's happening," she argues, yet her voice is still so gentle and calm.

"Oh, so what then? Is he moving here? Does he want Ava every other weekend and some holidays or something? Because that's not what you just said," I say.

"I just need time to feel the situation out and figure out what's best for Ava. She'll always come first, Hawk. Before you, before us, before anything," she says.

"That's what I'm asking you to consider. Damn, Drew, can't you see that?" I shrug my shoulders, my arms falling to my sides.

She walks toward me, taking slow, measured steps, like one wrong move could unravel us both. She's light as a feather, reaching up and brushing her knuckles across my cheek and jaw and finally my lips. I press my hand against hers, pressing my face into her palm as I shut my eyes.

"I just need the week to figure this out," she says. "Do you trust me?"

I nod slowly, gazing into her honey eyes for as long as she'll stand there and let me. I've surrendered to her. My inability to change or control any of this hits me in the face like a brick.

"I've already talked to Will to arrange taking the week off," she says.

I swallow, realizing what she's telling me without saying it. *I won't see her all week.*

"You can text me, though," she says.

I nod, knowing if I open my mouth I'll beg. I also know that sending her texts won't feel like enough.

Drew reaches up and presses the softest kiss to my lips then pulls away just as fast, walking past me and out the door without another word spoken between us.

An emptiness spreads through me, something I can't quite explain. I feel like I've been split open, like someone scooped out half of my insides and then just walked out that door.

The worst of it is an overwhelming fear that maybe she won't come back at all.

AIN'T NO MAN
DREW

The conversation I had with Hawk felt brutal but was necessary in the end. There was no way I could do what I needed to do this week and see him every day or have him around. It would only make things more difficult. So after the talk with him, and telling Curtis he could shove it up his b-hole if he thought he could stay at the apartment, I had to sit down with Ava and explain in further detail what was going on.

It's not a conversation a mother should have to have with her daughter, especially at her age. But she's mature, and seemed to understand most of what I had to explain to her. *Yes, Dad's in town. No, we're not back together. Yes, you can see him if you want. No, Hawk won't be around this week. No, Dad doesn't live here. No, we're not moving.*

Or at least I don't think so.

When I tuck her in and say goodnight to her, she seems okay and willing to see her father. Which is more than I can say for myself. But aside from the few minutes I left them alone here at the apartment so I could go talk to Hawk, it's my mission not to give him much more freedom in regard to being alone with her. At least not for quite a while.

The next morning, he comes over bright and early because he wants to drive Ava to school. He comes bearing coffee and breakfast, which I can only assume is his attempt at a peace offering.

I take a sip, actually relieved for this one thing he did, because coffee is a morning necessary. But I immediately spit it out in the sink. "That's just wrong," I say, wiping at the coffee spittle running down my chin.

"You don't like hazelnut?" he asks.

"I've never liked it," I say, and there's shock written across both our faces. Mine, because he clearly doesn't know me. And his, likely for the same reason.

"Huh, must've forgot," he says, shrugging it off. He turns to Ava with food in his hands. "Here, princess," he says, setting the food down in front of her.

Ava looks up at him, her lips pressed together.

"What's wrong?" he asks.

I walk over and immediately see the problem. "She hates onion bagels is the problem. And sausage. Always a plain bagel. Always bacon," I say, rolling my eyes and removing the sandwich from Ava's plate. "Here," I say to her, handing her some donuts. "Have a couple of these."

"I'm sorry," Curtis says, playing with his watch and checking the time.

"Busy? Have somewhere to be?" I scoff.

"No, no, of course not," he says.

I wish there was a way to accurately describe my frustration with Curtis in this moment. It isn't like Ava and I left years ago.

It hasn't been that long at all. And none of this is new information; our likes and dislikes haven't changed. We're not brand new
fucking people. Which makes me question just how much he
paid attention to anything when we were an actual family.

Ava collects her backpack, and I go with Curtis to drive her to
school. All the while, she looks at me frequently for assurance.
Curtis tries to initiate conversation with her, but it's stiff and
awkward for everyone involved.

On the nights Hawk stays over or when we stay at his place,
he talks to Ava with ease. They laugh and draw together. It's
natural, comfortable. Something tells me these noted differences
between Curtis and Hawk, and how Ava interacts with each of
them, are only the beginning.

Part of me wonders if it's fair to compare the two men. Then,
another part of me says *hell yes it is*, and I like that part better. So I
compare the shit out of them.

I glance at Curtis as we drive Ava, really taking in his facial
features. His mossy brown hair isn't quite straight or curly.
Though, it's not handsome waves either. It's just, sort of, there,
like a football helmet.

His eyes are a foggy blue, nothing special. Not electric, like
Hawk's, and they certainly don't light up. His body is...*okay*. No
tattoos. And that's all I have to say about that.

Tattoos were never a thing I noticed before. Their presence or
lack thereof never made it to the pros or cons list. Until now.
Looking at his bare arms and the naked double-chin forming
where his neck should be, I can confidently say tattoos are now
in the pros list. And bodies without them...well, meh.

We drop Ava off and continue driving. He doesn't know it yet,
but I'm directing him to the tattoo shop. He did ask to see where

I work, after all. I just didn't offer up what I did. I figure it'll be a fun little surprise for him.

"So, I see you've got a new tattoo," he says, ironically.

"Yep," I say.

"And what prompted you to do that?" he asks.

I shrug, not wishing to get into some debate about why you should or shouldn't get tattooed. "I wanted to."

"I see. Could it be the influence of that friend you have?" he asks.

The way Curtis keeps punctuating the word *friend* when he talks about Hawk is really starting to piss me off.

"Well, he is the one who did it," I say, giving him a satisfied look.

"I don't know what's come over you. Maybe it's living in the city, or being around people you shouldn't, but my Drew never would've done that," he says.

"Your Drew is dead," I bite out, my hand coming to rest on the handle of the shop door as I look back at him.

"What are we doing here?" he asks.

"You wanted to see where I work, right?" I ask, pushing the door open and hearing the familiar bell ding overhead.

"You work…*here*?" he asks, twirling his finger through the air like he's pointing at everything all at once. The emphasis and dismay he places on the word *here* amuses me.

"Yep," I say, a satisfied grin spreading over my lips.

Curtis looks around at the tattoo flash on the wall and toward the booths in the back, then comes eye to eye with Will at the front counter. She doesn't look pleased.

"Will, this is Curtis. I told you about him on the phone," I say, with my biggest and fakest smile planted on my face.

"Right, the ex-husband who's swooped in to further fuck up your life," she says, putting her hand out to shake his.

"Something like that," I say.

Curtis says, "Well, that's hardly—"

"Who's this?" Hanson says.

"Oh, this is Curtis. My ex-husband," I say, my tone flat.

Hanson steps closer, crossing his arms over his chest, running his eyes over Curtis. "I don't like the way he looks," Hanson says.

I start laughing, despite my best efforts. Well, maybe not *best*, but I tried a little.

"Who the fuck is this guy?" Avery says, stepping out from the back. *Just in time.*

"This is Curtis. Drew's ex-husband," Hanson says.

Avery takes his turn glaring at Curtis while I lean against the front counter with Will, thoroughly enjoying the show.

"What's wrong with his face?" Avery asks Hanson, as if Curtis can't hear them, like they can't simply ask him directly.

"My face?" Curtis tries to ask, rubbing his chin.

"I don't know, dude. It looks sort of flabby, like someone let the air out of the bottom half," Hanson says to Avery, ignoring Curtis.

"Maybe if he got some tattoos on this part of his neck, it would camouflage it a little," Avery replies to Hanson, pointing at the front of Curtis's neck.

"Drew, can we go?" Curtis says to me, clearly over this little game the two men are playing at his expense. Meanwhile, I'm in heaven.

"Drew?" Hawk's voice travels from behind the others, his body appearing in the hallway as he steps out of the office.

"Hey there, I was just showing Curtis where I work," I say, winking.

Hawk walks toward us all near the front desk, pushing past Avery and Hanson and coming to the front of the group. "So, you want to get a tattoo?" he asks Curtis.

"No, that's not why I'm here," Curtis replies.

"Come on, I'll even do it on the house. A friends and family discount. I'll give you something to really go with your personality," Hawk says.

"And what would that be?" Curtis asks.

"How about a little dick? I've done one before. It's not hard," he says.

I laugh again, as does the rest of the gang. Because we're all grown children and Hawk just made a flaccid dick joke I'm fairly certain flew right over Curtis's head.

Curtis squints at Hawk, his beady eyes shrinking even smaller. Avery and Hanson snicker behind Hawk, making no attempt to shield their reactions.

"Let's go Drew," Curtis says.

I wave bye to all of them, longing to give Hawk a different kind of goodbye but knowing now isn't the time. I have to show Curtis he doesn't belong here. And I don't mean in this city. I mean with me. Or Ava. *Not anymore.*

I don't know what's happened between the moment I left him and now, but I've changed—*we've* changed. I'm not the person I was before. I'm not the Drew he knew. I'm different now, and proud of the person I've become.

I'll just have to make him see.

100 BAD DAYS
HAWK

This is by far the most miserable I've been in years. I haven't seen Drew in two days. Not since she brought Curtis by the shop. I know she did that on purpose just to fuck with him, and it was pretty funny. But now, I just miss her.

Seeing her then made me want to rip his throat out like that scene in *Roadhouse*. *Also, RIP Patrick Swayze.* I had the violent urge mostly because it's his fault I haven't seen her. Actually, it's totally and completely all of his fault I haven't seen her. She's texted me a couple of times, but it's been very brief and very casual. I don't know if that's better or worse than no communication at all.

So here I am, drinking with the guys again, in an effort to keep myself from driving to her place and rearranging his soft pudgy face. *God.* I didn't even think to ask if he's staying there in the apartment with them. *Would he be sleeping on the couch? He better fucking be sleeping on the couch.* This is the worst.

Avery snaps his fingers in front of my face, abruptly pulling me from my thoughts. "Snap out of it, man," he says.

"Sorry." I pout. What's worse is I know I'm pouting.

"What did I tell you the last time I was here?" he asks.

"What do you mean?" I reply.

"I mean, this is hardly showing up for her," he says.

"This isn't the same thing," I say, waving off his advice.

"Sure it is. What did I say? I said, even when she doesn't need you or doesn't want you around, you have to show up for her, you have to be there," he says.

I take a big gulp of my whiskey and throw my head back against my couch. He's wrong. *Isn't he? How do I show up for someone who needs me to stay away? Is staying away a form of showing up?* That's too confusing to even think about.

I shove away those thoughts and focus on the fact that the week she asked for to deal with him is almost over and I'll know what the hell is going on. I'll have answers.

The thought of losing her and Ava permanently takes my breath away. Like someone sucker punched me in the solar plexus.

I check my phone the way I have been every hour on the hour but there's nothing there.

"You love her, don't you?" Hanson asks, studying my face as I put my phone down.

"Yes." I breathe out a heavy sigh.

"Holy shit, dude," he says.

"I know," I say.

"Okay, man, I'm only going to say this once," Avery says. "But if you really love that girl and you really want to be with her, then you're going to have to show her. Like really show her. Make her see it, feel it, believe it. Like beyond any doubts she might be holding onto."

"Mhmm," Hanson says, nodding his head up and down. His coal black eyes literally feel like they're looking right through me.

"I'm going to bed. You guys can crash here if you want. Couch is open. Spare bedroom. You know where the blankets are," I say.

It's not that I'm intentionally pushing away their advice and suggestions, but I can't think about it anymore. It's too much. I stand and walk into my room, taking a seat at the foot of the bed. I press my palms into my eye sockets and huff.

Maybe they're right. Maybe I need to *grand gesture* this thing. Maybe I need to show up and kick Curtis's ass and—*no, that's not right.* Maybe I need to show up and propose to her and—*no, that's not right either.* Maybe I should show up and tell her I love her while she's fucking awake. That might be okay. But I don't want to do it in front of that fuckface. *God.* I'm going to have to wait until this stupid shit is over.

I slam myself back on my bed and take out my phone, staring at the empty screen. Still no word from her. I decide, at the very least, I'm allowed to text her. I don't think I have to wait until she texts me first.

Me: I know I didn't ask this before but it's bugging me.

Drew: What?

Me: Is he staying there?

Drew: God no. He's in a hotel.

I breathe a sigh of relief and no longer feel like I have to vomit.

Drew: Gross. Lol.

Me: I'm glad you think so.

Drew: I miss you.

Ugh. My heart.

Me: I miss you too.

Me: This is almost over right?

Drew: I think so.

Me: I can just disappear him, you know.

Drew: OMG I don't even want to know what that means. Lol

Me: Hanson knows people.

Drew: Baby Hanson? Knows people for disappearing??

Me: You don't want to know.

Drew: You're right.

Me: I guess I should get some sleep.

Drew: Me too.

Me: It's hard without my straitjacket.

Drew: Lol goodnight <3

I pull off my clothes and slide under the blanket, adjusting my pillows again and again. I even try to scrunch one up and make it the little spoon, but it doesn't work. I'm hopeless. I've never had this much trouble falling asleep in my life.

Is this actually what love is? Because if so, it's stupid.

No, this is worry. Right. Worry, not love. Worry for the future, what's at stake. What I stand to lose. *How the fuck am I gonna lose to a fuckface like Curtis?* No, I decide. No way. No matter what, I won't go out like that. Not to him, anyway. If a better man comes along, well, we'll talk about it. But no way am I going down against that man. If you can even call him a man.

I close my eyes and think of Drew. Her perfect body pressed against mine. If I concentrate hard enough, I can almost feel her lips on mine.

What an empty way to fall asleep.

THE PRETENDER
DREW

No matter what happens, today is the day Curtis has got to go. Even if I have to call in a favor to Hanson and *disappear him,* as Hawk says. In all seriousness, I make a mental note to ask more about that later as I sit on Ava's bed with her.

Curtis is on his way over, fully expecting some sort of answer from me. He seems to think this week *went swimmingly,* as he put it.

"How did you like having your dad here?" I ask Ava.

Ava looks down at her lap but doesn't say a word.

"You can be honest with me, Ava. It's just the two of us. You can always tell me the truth," I say, encouraging her unfiltered thoughts and opinions.

She looks up at me, tears brimming her eyes. "It's like he doesn't even know me."

"What do you mean?" I ask her, brushing her hair behind her ear.

"He doesn't know anything I like to eat. He doesn't know

anything I like to do or play with. He doesn't know my favorite color or song. He doesn't know me at all," she says, her voice trembling.

"He could get to know you again," I offer.

"It doesn't feel like he wants to," she says.

"Why do you say that?" I ask, my heart constricting a little more with each tear she sheds.

"Because even when I told him stuff or reminded him what I liked, he didn't care. He didn't apologize or remember the next time," she says, tears beginning to stream down her face.

And that pretty much seals the deal for me. Maybe if Ava had wanted him around, maybe if she'd been willing to let him back in, hell, maybe if he'd even shown even a drop of sincerity, this might be going differently. But the truth is, I think he got bored. Or maybe desperate. Maybe whatever woman he was with left him and he just didn't want to be alone. Maybe he thought we were a safe bet. But we're not going back to him. Not now and not ever. My mind is 100% made up about that.

I brush the tears from Ava's cheeks and kiss her forehead. Then, I head into the living room to wait for him. I wring my hands together, nervous for the conversation I'm about to have with him. He's never been a particularly violent man, so I'm not worried for my physical safety. But if the past showed me anything, it's that Curtis can be downright vindictive in many other ways.

When he knocks on the door, however, something inside me clicks. The momma bear in me, who wants nothing more than to protect her cub at all costs, takes over. I flick the door open and wave him in, not bothering to look at him.

"Well," he says.

"I'm going to stop you right there. I've got some things to say," I say. I don't want him to steer the conversation. Not this time. I'm in charge now.

"Oh, all right. You first then, I guess," he says. Curtis sits on the couch but I stay standing.

"You don't care about us. I know you say you do but this week has made it very clear that you don't. So what's her name? Or I guess I should ask, what *was* her name?" I snap.

"Who?" he asks, his eyes shifting back and forth a tad too dramatic to feel sincere.

"Whoever you were seeing up until she left and you panicked. And don't lie," I warn.

"I was seeing a woman named Patricia. But that's not why—"

"Yes it is. We both know it ended and you panicked and that's the only reason you're here. You don't even remember what Ava likes and doesn't like. And despite her telling you all week, you keep ignoring her," I say, breathless now.

"I can try harder," he says.

"No you can't, because this is who you are. This is always who you were. And we're not going with you," I say, crossing my arms over my chest.

Curtis chews on the inside of his jaw, eyes squinting at me, sizing me up. If he thinks I'm bluffing he can try to call it, but it won't end well for him.

"Well, that's disappointing. I wanted to do this the easy way," he says.

"What do you mean?" I ask.

"I mean, you can both come back with me and we can all be one big happy family, or I'll have no choice but to file a petition with the courts for full custody," he says.

"Are you crazy? On what grounds?" I shriek.

"Well, look at you. This tiny apartment, your pathetic little job. And look at the company you keep. All those tattooed lowlifes. You're clearly unfit and putting our child at risk," he says.

I swallow hard, knowing as an attorney he's done worse and proven more ridiculous accusations in past cases.

"You wouldn't," I say, trying not to let my voice shake.

"I think you know I will." A sinister smile spreads over his lips.

The panic in my throat threatens to bubble over in the form of vomit. I've seen ruthless courtroom Curtis in action. And I know he would do it, just to punish me.

A knock at the door interrupts our conversation and I rush to open it, panic and fear gripping me.

"Hawk," I say, surprised. "What are you doing here?"

"Is he still here?" Hawk asks, and I nod. "Look, I can't wait any longer. I shouldn't have waited at all. I should've been here."

"Oh, is your little friend here?" Curtis calls, and Hawk walks past me toward him.

"Yeah, I don't think I'll be going this time," Hawk says to Curtis.

"Well, I think I'll be leaving soon anyway. Seems Drew wants to stay here." A *tsk* and then, "I need to get back home. Lots of paperwork to file," Curtis says, hinting at his intentions.

"Going to just give up all your parental rights, then?" Hawk asks.

"Oh no, quite the opposite. Seems I'll have full custody of Ava in no time," Curtis says, looking down at his cuticles, not a care in the world.

I can feel the chunks rising in my throat. A sheen of sweat has formed on my forehead and I might actually pass out. I put my hand on Hawk's forearm just to steady myself.

"What's that now?" Hawk asks, clenching his fists.

"Well, I just don't think this is a suitable environment for my daughter. So I'll be taking her," Curtis clarifies.

Hawk narrows his gaze. If looks could kill, Curtis would be dead.

Curtis swallows, taking half a step back and straightening his collar.

"Yeah, you go file that paperwork," Hawk says. "That's a good idea. But you should know something about me first."

"Yeah? What's that? Gonna threaten to kick my ass or something?" Curtis mocks. "Feel like going to jail? Because I'll press charges."

"Oh, I'm sure you would. But no, nothing so juvenile. But here's the deal, fuckface. I've been here. Every day. Granted, it hasn't been all that long. Not yet. But I'm the one who cares about them. I'm the one who wants to fight for them. And that's what I'll do. I'll hire the best lawyer in the country. Way better than you. Because I've got a lot of money and a lot of time. And by the end of it, you'll be paying out of your ass in alimony and child support costs. And visitation? Forget about it. You'll be paying so much, you'll be the one living in a tiny apartment," Hawk says. Then he comes to my side and wraps his arm around my waist.

I'm so shocked by his words, I'm speechless. I couldn't form a sentence if I wanted to. I stare up at his face, awestruck.

Curtis has a similar reaction. "Please. You have money?" he asks.

"Looks can be very deceiving, Curtis," Hawk says. "Take you for example. You look nice enough but inside you're just a prick. Believe me or don't. I dare you."

Curtis swallows again, rubbing his palms down the sides of his slacks. Suddenly I want to burn all my slacks, never wear a pair again. "Well, this all feels so unnecessary," Curtis says.

"Oh it does, huh?" Hawk asks. "Would you like to go ahead and have a change of heart?"

Curtis clears his throat, not yet ready to admit his defeat. "I'll be in touch," he says, and then, he walks out the door.

A wave of relief washes over me. Hawk stares in the direction of the door for a little while longer, probably making sure Curtis isn't going to walk back in.

When the coast seems clear, my knees buckle beneath me and I become a sobbing mess on the ground.

WHATEVER IT TAKES
HAWK

As soon as the door closes behind Curtis, Drew collapses—her body shaking, sobs escaping her. I drop to her side, wrapping myself around her. "Shhh, it's okay, it's over," I whisper.

Drew sniffles and keeps her head buried in my neck for several minutes. Though, I'd have let her do it as long as she needed to. I want her to know she can always rely on me, even just to be here if she needs to cry.

"This week has been so awful," she says. "I'm so sorry."

"Don't be sorry," I say. "It's not your fault."

"I shouldn't have even entertained the idea. I should've made him leave as soon as he showed up," she says between sobs.

Part of me wishes she would've, but I'll never say she should've. I know it was an impossible situation for her. She had to make her own decisions, in her own time.

"It's over now," I assure her.

"He says he'll be in touch. What if he really tries to take Ava?" she asks.

"I won't let that happen," I say.

"But you don't know Curtis. He's a powerful lawyer," she says.

"I'll find one that's more powerful than him." I shrug, ultimately unconcerned by his threats. Even still, I understand why she would be.

To have someone in a position of power threaten to take your child away has to be unbearably frightening. The thought of losing that child to someone who's only doing it to hurt you certainly has to be a pain like nothing I've ever felt.

We sit together in silence for a while longer, holding each other, listening to the other breathe in and out. I close my eyes and realize just how much I've missed her this week. I seriously can't imagine doing that again.

"Listen. What I'm about to say is going to sound really crazy, but hear me out," I start.

Drew pulls her head up from my chest, looking me in the eyes. "Okay…"

"Move in with me," I say, more a statement than a question.

"What?" she says, her eyes growing wide. She shuffles, sitting up straight, and stares at me like I've lost my mind. And maybe I have.

"I know, I said it's going to sound crazy, but just think about it," I say, attempting to play to her rational side. "You'll be closer to work. Plus, Curtis won't be able to say you live in a tiny apartment anymore."

"Are you trying to use convenience and scare tactics to get me to move in with you?" she asks, laughing.

"That depends. It is working?" I ask.

"I don't think close proximity to work is a good reason to move in with someone," she says.

I'm not denying the fact that she has a good point, but I'm also not giving up. "Well, I have other reasons too," I say.

"Okay, I'm listening," she says.

I breathe in deep, clearing my throat. "I love Ava," I say. "And I love you." I reach up to rub my knuckles across her jaw and it trembles beneath my touch.

"You do?" she asks.

"Without a doubt," I say.

I watch the muscles in her neck work up and down as she swallows, trying to hold back the tears from falling. She presses her forehead to my chest so hard I feel her warm breath on my skin through my T-shirt.

I don't know how long she's quiet. It could be thirty seconds or five full minutes. It all feels the same, like time is standing still as I watch the woman I love wrestle with this new information.

She tilts her head up, finally looking at me again, and I hold my breath. "I love you too," she says.

My heart feels like it collapses in on itself then, because waiting to hear her response was so agonizing, I didn't know what to expect. And now that she's said it back, I feel over-whelmed with relief and happiness. I might start crying myself if I'm not careful. I don't remember a time in my life I was this happy.

"But are you sure we should move in together?" she asks.

I consider her question for a long moment. "Do you want to do this again? This thing where we go days without seeing each other or nights apart or any of this?" I ask, and she shakes her head. "I don't either," I tell her. "So, I say as long as Ava is okay with it, and you want to, then it's the best idea I've had since... that time in eleventh grade when I superglued my brother's thumbs together."

Drew laughs, and I like making her laugh, because I love the sound of it. "Okay," she says.

"Okay?" I repeat. "Okay, like, you'll move in?"

"Yes," she says.

I wrap my arms around her and pull her to me so tightly I might break both our ribs but it'll be worth it.

"What's going on out here?" Ava asks.

We straighten ourselves, standing up from the floor and moving to the couch.

"Ava, come here," Drew says. "Hawk has a question for you."

"What?" she asks, stepping toward us.

"I was just asking your mom if maybe the two of you would want to move in with me?" I ask her.

Ava's eyes brighten as she looks from my face to her mom's and back again. "For real?" she asks.

"Yep. You can cuddle with the dogs all you want," I say.

"Yes!" she exclaims, jumping onto us.

I begin to fluff up her hair and she giggles as she always does, then stops.

"Wait," Ava says. "I have a couple of questions."

"Okay, shoot," I say.

Drew looks at me and shrugs her shoulders, so apparently we're both unsure what they could possibly be.

"What kind of breakfast sandwich do I like?" Ava asks me.

I keep eye contact, because for whatever reason, her face seems quite serious. "Always bacon. Always a plain bagel," I say.

"And what's my favorite color?" she asks.

"Purple," I reply.

"Favorite thing to do in the whole world?" she asks.

"Draw, of course," I say. I look over at Drew, whose face is soft and understanding.

"Okay, we can move in," Ava says.

With that, she skips off back to her room because she says she needs to start packing, and Drew lays her head back down on my chest.

"What was that all about?" I ask.

"Nothing, she just had to be sure," Drew says.

I nod, satisfied that I passed whatever test she just administered.

Drew doesn't know it yet, but I'm calling movers first thing tomorrow and paying extra for expedited service. I'm also going to speak with the contractors on the expansion of the shop, to expand my loft over the new space too, virtually doubling our home in size. *Our home.* It feels both strange and wonderful to think about.

I never thought in a million years I'd be doing this. I never guessed I'd have a family outside of the one I made with Bird's Eye. If I've learned anything, it's that people change. I've definitely changed.

Something tells me many more changes lie ahead, and that's okay. I'll be ready for them. *We'll* be ready for them. I don't know what the future holds, but I do know who I want to face it with.

"I love you, psycho," Drew whispers to me.

"I love you, too, my little straitjacket," I say.

And for now, that's enough.

EPILOGUE I
FIRST DAY OF MY LIFE

DREW

When you get married, you always think to yourself: *This is it. This is the one. Forever and ever. This is my always.* No one is ever thinking about the next one or what they'll do if this one doesn't work out.

And then, for whatever reason, when the first one ends, almost everyone swears they'll never do it again. *That's it. No way. I'm done. I'll be alone forever before I go through that again.* I have to admit, I whispered all those same sentiments to myself.

So imagine my surprise when Hawk proposed to me on our one-year anniversary. Ava helped him pick out a gorgeous antique princess cut diamond set in platinum. But of course, they didn't do that until after he got Ava's permission to ask me.

Her only reply was, *"What took so long?"* Of course, that's how nine-year-olds are.

The wedding was brilliant. I wore a sleeveless champagne dress, all lace with the back cut out. It showed off all my new tattoos really well. I still don't have nearly as many as anyone else in the shop, but I've acquired a few over the course of dating a tattoo artist.

Ava stood up there, not as a flower girl, but as of equal importance. Because Hawk wasn't just marrying me, he was marrying us. He was making a promise to both of us. Granted, different promises, but just as significant.

I watch him walk up the beach, back to our chairs, with two drinks in his hand. Our honeymoon is nearly over and soon we'll be back in cold weather. So we're soaking up all the sun and sand we can while we're still here.

Will generously agreed to watch Ava while we're gone. And let me tell you, ten days of kid-free time, is nothing short of amazing. But as the trip comes to an end, I realize how much I'm starting to miss her.

"You know," Hawk says as he sits down in his lounge chair, "I'm starting to miss Ava."

I laugh and tell him, "I was just thinking the same thing."

"Two more days and we will be back in Louisville," he says.

Then he hands me my drink, complete with pieces of fruit and a colorful umbrella sticking out of the top. I definitely want to learn how to make whatever this drink is at home. It's so tasty and sweet, you can't even taste the alcohol. Which means I drink about five of them before I realize I'm drunk and sometimes Hawk gets the sloppy sex. But he doesn't complain. *Sex is sex, right?*

I look out over the water and then down at my wedding bands. Hawk's fingers are laced in mine and I'm fairly certain I could stay like this forever.

"What are you thinking?" he asks.

"I'm thinking we should go back to our room and make the good sex," I say.

Hawk chokes on the sip of his beer and looks at me, laughing. "I really can't argue with that suggestion," he says.

While he grabs our towels, I make a run for it. Luckily, the patio doors to our villa are only a few hundred feet from where we're sitting. I run up the couple of steps onto the deck and pull open the sliding glass door, slipping my flipflops off and then walking inside.

We've spent the majority of this trip nearly naked or completely naked. I'm wearing a small black bikini and he's wearing black swimming trunks, so it doesn't exactly take us long to undress.

We slide between the soft, thin sheets, seeing as we abandoned the comforter on the floor the day we arrived and never bothered to put it back on.

Hawk presses his lips to mine and I eagerly part them, giving permission to his tongue. Just over a year in, and still, I'm so hungry for him. Just over a year in, and still, my body aches for him the same way it did the very first time.

I grip his back as he pushes into me, rocking his hips against mine, his tattooed torso rigid against me. He hooks an arm under one of my legs and pulls it up, splitting my body in half.

I moan against his mouth as he pushes deeper. "I love you," I whisper.

"I love you, too," he says, half-growling.

Before I know it, I'm spinning with pleasure, an orgasm building inside me.

"Come for me," he whispers against my throat.

His command is all it takes for me to unravel. I love it when he does that.

Then we lie in bed together, panting and curling into each other.

"I don't know about you, but I could go for a nap," he says.

"You're so old," I tease.

"Not too old to impregnate you, I hope," he says.

My head shoots up and I stare at him, bewildered. "Are you serious?"

"I mean, I've been thinking about it. You haven't thought about it?" he says.

"Of course I've thought about it, I just didn't think you wanted kids. Or at least any more or any of your own," I say.

"Well, people change, babe." He shrugs.

"God, you're going to be really old though. Like, gray-haired and stuff," I tease.

"Wow, thanks," he says, slapping my ass. "I'm only like three years older than you, thank you very much."

"Yeah, but three years is practically a lifetime," I joke. "I guess that means I shouldn't drink any more fruity umbrella drinks. Or take my birth control pills."

"We can wait a while if you want?" he asks.

"Maybe just one more fruity umbrella drink," I say, giggling.

Hawk squeezes me tightly, pressing me further to his chest.

Sometimes life is really strange. It doesn't work out the way you planned. It's not as clean cut as you thought it would be. Sometimes it gets a little messy. But sometimes it's better when it goes off script.

Sometimes it gives you what you never knew you wanted.

EPILOGUE II

FELL IN LOVE WITH A GIRL

HAWK

To be clear, we never heard from Curtis. Not in the days after he left. Or the months after Drew and Ava moved in with me. Not after I proposed or after we got married. We didn't hear from him as we welcomed our son, Knox, into the world and Ava became a big sister.

We didn't even hear from Curtis after we had attorneys serve him papers of our own. *No, not for his money.* I didn't need whatever measly child support they'd make him pay. I had bigger plans than that.

I walk up the front of the courtroom steps, Ava's hand in mine and Drew's hand in her other. Knox is strapped to the front of Drew, fast asleep. We walk through metal detectors, wait in lines, go up stairs, navigate to the family court wing, and wait again, this time for our turn. We sit on a bench, our attorney sitting to the left of us.

I scan the room, noticing Curtis didn't even bother to show up today.

As our names are called, we rise, and then we're directed to walk forward and stand in a certain spot. The judge flips through a stack of papers.

"This matter is in regard to Ava Ashby?" the judge asks, looking up from the stack of files in front of him.

"Yes, Your Honor," our attorney replies.

"You've submitted that the biological father has signed over all legal and custodial rights, rendering him no longer morally responsible or financially obligated to her, is that correct?" he asks.

"Yes, Your Honor," our attorney says again.

"And a Mister Hawk Anthony Tanner is present and wishes to legally adopt Ava Ashby as his own daughter, is that correct?" The judge looks at me and then to my attorney.

I swallow hard, squeezing Ava's hand. She looks up at me, a mix of fear and excitement in her eyes. I wink at her, to reassure her that everything's going to be okay.

"That's correct, Your Honor. He's married to Ava's mother," our attorney says.

The judge looks over all of us, Ava last. "Are you Ava?" he asks, his voice softening as he does so.

She looks up at me again, and I nod. "Yes, sir," she says.

"Can I ask you a question, Ava?" the judge says, and Ava nods again. "Do you want this man to be your dad?" he asks her.

Ava looks up at me, a small genuine smile plastered on her face. Then she says, "Yes, sir. He's the best."

The judge chuckles at her answer, and so do I. My heart swells and there's a lump in my throat the size of a Mack truck.

"And would you like to be Ava Tanner now?" he asks.

"Yes, sir," she says excitedly.

The judge straightens the papers in front of him and looks at a few more pieces of information. "Very well, then. By the power vested in me by the State of Kentucky, you are hereby Ava Tanner and that, little lady, is your dad," he says, closing his statement to her with a wink.

Ava turns and jumps to try to hug me. I bend and scoop her up, wrapping my arms around her.

"Does this mean I can call you Dad now?" she asks.

"Of course, kid. I wouldn't have it any other way," I say.

Drew leans in, tears in her eyes, and presses a kiss to my cheek. "Thank you," she says.

"For what?" I ask.

"For making us a whole family," she says.

I look down at Knox sleeping against her, his wisps of black hair floating as if gravity doesn't exist.

"Drew, before you and Ava, I didn't even know I could have this. I didn't make a whole anything. You guys did," I tell her.

She leans up and kisses my mouth.

"Gross, guys," Ava says.

I sit Ava back down and she gently strokes the tiny hands of her baby brother. I stare at Drew, knowing she made all of this possible. I can't imagine my life any different than this one.

If you'd told me a few years ago this would be my future, I would've laughed in your face and told you to get the hell out of my shop. But now, I'm an old, soft, and changed man.

But not so soft anyone should ever consider fucking with my family. Because I will definitely disappear their ass.

THE END

ACKNOWLEDGMENTS

So we meet again, acknowledgments. My arch nemesis. Ugh. Fine, fine. I'll do it.

Jen Rogue. You are without a doubt one of the only constants I've had in my life for a very long time. I don't know what I would do without you. Your presence motivates me, encourages me, and is a driving force for me. I would definitely disappear someone for you.

Christina Slaylen Hart. When I'm having a bad day, a good day, an unbelievable day, you're someone I can always count on to just be there for me. As my editor, you've pushed me to be a better writer, a better storyteller. As a friend, you've pushed me to examine life from a different perspective. I would 100% disappear someone for you.

For my children, Kali and Kaden. You still just eat all my food and live in my house rent free, so thanks for nothing. For my bonus child, Mattie. You came into my life under sad circumstances. The road was tough, but I'm glad you're with me. I can't imagine life without you now. You eat a lot of food, though. Let's calm down. Only a few more years until you can drive and go to the store for me, so, win! Don't worry, I've already disappeared people for you guys. Just kidding...

For Chris, that guy who sleeps in my bed. I love you and stuff. Thanks for being my Hawk. You take care of three kids who aren't yours every single day and you only complain sometimes. But like, normal parent complaints. Not complaints about their existence. Thanks for swiping right on my Tinder profile. You're the okayest. Definitely a little psycho. I don't need to disappear people for you because you're the person I call when I need someone disappeared so I'll just stop talking now in case the FBI sees this.

For every single person, fellow author, friend, blogger, reviewer, anyone who read and loved Hawk as much as I do, thank you. Your hype for him gives me life. Please shove him in the faces of all your friends until the end of time. If you guys ever need anyone disappeared, I know a guy.

And last but definitely not least, my dogs, Loki and Ghost. Thank you for all the cuddles, for constantly nudging your face into my laptop when it was on my lap, for needing to go outside to pee on our fence every five minutes, and for needing treats around the clock. Without you guys distracting me on a regular basis, I would get way more writing done. And, as an author, I can't tell you how awful that would be. Good thing you don't know what sarcasm is. I also assume you don't have a list of enemies you need disappeared? There's nothing I can do about the mailman, get over it.

ALSO BY KAT SAVAGE

Novels:

A Fighting Chance (A Chance At Love, #1)

One More Chance (A Chance At Love, #2)

Taking A Chance (A Chance At Love, #3)

With This Lie

For Now

Poetry:

Counting Backwards From Gone

I Hope This Makes You Uncomfortable

This is How I Die

Throes

Redamancy

Anchors & Vacancies

Mad Woman

Learning To Speak

Letters from a Dead Girl

Kat Savage resides in Louisville, Kentucky with her family of heathens. She's Slytherin, House Stark, and 99% sure her ancestors were pagan Viking Danes.

Kat Savage is a survivor of many ugly things and writes about them shamelessly in both poetry and novels.

Join her reader group on Facebook – Kat's MF Savages – and be the first to know all her secrets.

Kat Savage would love it if you reviewed her work on Goodreads because it's very helpful to her as an indie author.

Kat Savages loves and adores you. You are important to her. Always.

Find more about Kat Savage on www.thekatsavage.com or stalk her on social media:

Made in the USA
Middletown, DE
29 June 2021